"Sarah Ladipo Manyika's *Like a Mule Bringing Ice Cream to the Sun...* the rare sort of book that, from the instant you pick it up, you know that you will be privy to the most intimate secrets. It is as if Dr. Morayo Da Silva is speaking directly into your ear. A real life-force of a character whose honesty, warmth, · energy, and bravery in the face of inevitable loss springs forth on the page. Chekhov once said that the 'Russian loves to recall living, but he does not love living.' Da Silva manages, in her unique way, to love both, the remembering and life in the present tense. A beautiful, important new novel, and one that will continue to echo in a reader's mind for a long time after."

PETER ORNER, author of *Love and Shame and Love* and *Esther Stories*

"In this gorgeous and finely crafted book Sarah Manyika takes a sideways look at the lives of other people, lives that usually pass us and each other by, that when they touch may do so with no more than a glancing blow, but may also connect, as they do in *Like a Mule Bringing Ice Cream to the Sun,* tenderly, simply and sweetly. Sarah Manyika's novel shows ordinary people at their best. Uplifting!"

AMINATTA FORNA, author of *The Memory of Love, Ancestor Stones* and *The Devil that Danced on the Water*

"*Like a Mule Bringing Ice Cream to the Sun* follows the adventures of the fabulous Dr. Morayo, a woman dancing on the edge of old age. This remarkable story contains multitudes. It is a story of aging; the wry, stately voice of Dr. Morayo gives us a Grand Old Heroine for our times: mischievous, wise, fallible, feisty, and above all, strong. It is a love affair with San Francisco; a contrapuntal variety of voices and perspectives bring the city to eager, brimming life. And it is deeply political: speaking of a Nigerian woman's awesome sense of power and her simultaneous anguish at the depredations of her boko-haramed hometown. Wise, tender and beautifully voiced, *Like a Mule Bringing Ice Cream to the Sun* is a storytelling triumph."

LAVANYA SANKARAN, author of *The Red Carpet*

"A wonderfully constructed novel, always surprising and wrong-footing the reader at every turn and challenging one's assumptions about the Other. *Like a Mule Bringing Ice Cream to the Sun* is a delightful multi-helical reading experience that speaks to our times in insightful and pleasantly understated ways."

BRIAN CHIKWAVA, author of *Harare North*

Like a Mule Bringing Ice Cream to the Sun

By the same author
IN DEPENDENCE

Like a Mule Bringing Ice Cream to the Sun

Sarah Ladipo Manyika

CASSAVA REPUBLIC

Abuja - London

First published in 2016 by Cassava Republic Press
Abuja – London
www.cassavarepublic.biz

ISBN 978-1-911115-04-5
eISBN 978-1-911115-05-2

A CIP catalogue record for this book is available from the British Library.

'*Like a Mule Bringing Ice Cream to the Sun*' is taken from Mary Ruefle's poem, 'Donkey On'.

Book design by Allan Castillo Rivas.

Printed and bound by in Great Britain by Bell & Bain Ltd, Glasgow.

Distributed in Nigeria by Book River Ltd.

Distributed in the UK by Central Books Ltd.

For Us

I think we forget things if we have no one to tell them to.
RITESH JOGINDER BATRA, *The Lunchbox*

1

The place where I live is ancient. 'Old but sturdy,' our landlady tells us. 500 Belgrave is so strong, apparently, that it withstood the 1906 earthquake. 'Didn't even bust a single crack,' is what the landlady says. But between you and me, I wouldn't bet on history repeating itself. It's the reason why I live on the top floor, for if this building collapses, then at least they won't have far to dig me out. Of course, I don't wish any harm to my neighbours, especially not to the gentleman living just beneath me. As for the sullen woman on the ground floor who insists on calling me Mary because she finds Morayo too hard to pronounce, well that's another story. But I wish even her no harm. I'd like to imagine that when the big one strikes, we'd all be gathered at my place, enjoying a glass of wine, and we'd ride the whole thing out and live to tell the tale. But who knows, when the earth finally decides that it's tired of fidgeting and needs a proper stretch, I might be the one walking downstairs; if that's the case, then the only survivors will be my books – hundreds of them – to keep each other company.

Our building used to be a single family house, but now it's home to four separate units and I've been living in one of these for twenty years. This must be somewhat annoying to my poor landlady, for in this city of rent controls she could charge a new tenant much more than she charges me. Not that the apartment is anything spectacular mind you; it's just one small bedroom, kitchen, living room and bathroom. But it's the view that matters in San Francisco. And my view, oh yes, my view is *magnifique*.

When you stand at the kitchen sink you can see all the colourful houses of Haight Ashbury. And beyond these, the eucalyptus and pine forests of the Presidio that stretch across to the bay where, on a clear day, the waters shimmer azure blue. So I have no intention of moving, and the landlady must know that what she loses in rent, she gains by having someone reliable like me keeping a watchful eye on the property. For I, like this building, am ancient. Ancient if you're going by Nigerian standards, where I've outfoxed the female life expectancy by nearly two decades. And because I've lived in this building so long, I know all the comings and goings: such that on a morning like this, even before the mailman reaches the third floor, I've heard his footsteps. Li Wei is in the habit of taking the stairs two at a time, and when he arrives, I'm waiting for him. I wouldn't normally open the door in my dressing gown, but Li Wei is no stranger. Besides, this is a city where people walk their dogs and take their children to school in their pyjamas. So here I stand in my magenta silk dressing gown, barefoot and brushing the tops of my toes (those with toe rings) against the rough sisal of my 'welcome' mat.

'Hello Doctor Morayo, lots of mail for you today,' says Li Wei, presenting a neatened stack with such finesse that I'm reminded of a samurai bowing before his empress, palms extended, head slightly bent. 'The box was full,' he announces, looking puzzled until I smile and then he smiles because we both know there's nothing surprising about my mailbox being full. That's the way I leave it these days because I like him stopping by. We enjoy our little chats until it's time for Li Wei to return to work and he tips his postal hat to bid me good day. And out of respect for his kindness I always spend some minutes, after he's gone, sorting through the political party mailings, the letters from Amnesty and the Sierra Club. Occasionally, if a colourful postcard or a handwritten envelope falls from the pile, I get excited, thinking it might be from a friend, even though I know its usually just a prettier form of junk. Whatever happened to all those friends who used to send letters and postcards? Now people just zap off emails or no notes at all. And then, of course, so many friends have died. I flick, half-heartedly through *Granta* and *CAR*, and then stop to make myself a cup of tea into which I dip a ginger biscuit. Yes I know I'm procrastinating, and if I don't pay attention, I might be late with some bills. They don't give you much time to pay these days, but I don't let this trouble me. Once upon a time I was diligent, extraordinarily diligent, but life's too short to fuss over such small things. That at least is what I tell myself until the diligence, never truly lost, reappears, and I return to the post.

Today there's a letter from the Department of Motor Vehicles with forms attached. I glance at it, mentally checking *no, no,* and *no* to a history of high blood pressure, heart attacks, and diabetes. I presume the letter is routine. But hold on: it's my birthday soon so maybe that's what this is all about. Why when one gets to a 'certain age' must every reminder of a birthday carry a tinge of gloom? I look at the letter again and notice that the deadline for the reply was last week. Bother! Better call. I dial then cradle the phone between my ear and shoulder while unravelling my night-time cornrows, which I do on occasion to keep my hair tangle free. I don't mind waiting but the automated message gives me the option of receiving a return call without losing my place in line. How civilized! I leave my name and number, and now hands free, I unravel my last plait while pondering what to wear.

In my wardrobe sit a stack of brightly coloured fabrics. Some were gifts to myself, others presents from friends. Nowadays I enjoy wearing native attire much more than I used to, especially when it's sunny. Today I select a new Ankara in vibrant shades of pink and blue and then bring it to my nose. When I open the folds of cloth I'm delighted to find the smell of Lagos markets still buried in the cotton – diesel fumes, hot palm oil, burning firewood. The smell evokes the flamboyance and craziness of the megacity that once was mine in between my husband's diplomatic postings. It was a place of parties and traffic jams, the city of my husband's people: my many nephews, nieces and godchildren. I've often thought of returning to Lagos and sometimes dream that I've already moved back to this big crazy city where everyone calls me 'Auntie' or 'Mama';

the land of constant sunshine and daily theatre. I think of cousins and wonder what it might be like to reconnect with them, to live nearby. I've even contemplated living closer to Caesar, not because I miss him, particularly, but because we share memories of people and places that few others now remember. But even as I find myself searching the Internet for homes in Ikoyi, I know that I'm not likely to feel at home in such a crowded city. I remember how it floods during rainy season. I remember the power cuts and the unruly traffic, and I remember how few bookshops there are, how few cafes and museums. Deep down, I know that my desire to return comes more from nostalgia than a genuine longing to return. Those days of being able to deal with the daily headaches of Lagos life are gone. In any case it's to Jos, the city of my childhood, that I'd most like to return. But this is even more implausible. Jos used to be a place of serenity, of cool, plateau weather, not the anxious city it is today with the constant fears of random acts of violence. And now that my parents are gone and school friends have moved away or died, all that really remains are the memories.

I sigh, putting the original fabric aside and opting for another – this one gold and green, wafting eco-friendly, lavender-scented detergent. I wrap the material around my waist keeping my legs spread hip distance so as not to pull too tightly, then I wrap it again and finish with a secure tuck at the side. I choose a contrasting yellow material to wind around my hair and then check in the bathroom mirror, patting down the top of my Afro. Satisfied, I rub pink gloss on my lips and blot with a tissue. Off come my glasses and then two quick brushes of the eyebrows towards the temples with a baby toothbrush kept just for this purpose. I remember reading somewhere how this draws people's attention to the eyes. Eyes, said the apostle Matthew, are the lamp of the body. And if, according to something else I read recently, eyes are the one thing that never age, then this is a good thing. I remove my smudged glasses and clean them with warm soapy water, holding onto the rims as I was taught as a child.

I don't remember when I first started wearing glasses – it feels like a lifetime, but I do remember Kano Eye Hospital and the drive from Jos, which was a long and bumpy one, across dirt roads. The appointment, always scheduled for the following day, was also an all-day affair – from waiting on the wooden benches outside to sitting in the large optician's chair. The doctor liked to take his time choosing from drawers filled with rows of silver rimmed spheres, arranged neatly like biscuits in a tin. I used to imagine him having to choose between shortbread and ginger snaps before slotting the wafer thin lens into the bulky steel contraption placed on my nose. 'Better or worse?' he would ask, and sometimes it was better, sometimes worse. But always, I remember his breath smelling sweetly of mangos, which was how I came to believe he was poor. Mangos were free in Nigeria – anyone could pluck them off the trees, so much so that father would pay someone, during mango season, to collect the fruit so it wouldn't fall and rot. I've since wondered if the doctor suffered from diabetes. Wasn't sweet breath a sign of this disease? But perhaps the man just liked his mangos. And when it came time for him to peer into my eyes with his sharp yellow light, I used to find it impossible to do as instructed. Rather than stare at the bridge of his freckled nose, I preferred to look at my own eyes reflected in his where they appeared shiny and beautiful, like strawberry jam drops. It was always a mystery to me how my vision could be perfect up close, but so poor for distance. Then the phone rings.

'How can I help you?' I answer, smiling because the voice on the other end sounds familiar. 'Sunil?' I try placing the name.

'Oh yes, ma'am, this is the DMV and I'm just returning your call.'

'From the DMV,' I repeat. 'DMV, did you say? ... Oh, ... yes, of course.' I remember now but I've forgotten the good excuse I was intending to use. Now I just have to ask for an extension to the deadline.

'Well ma'am, give me one moment,' the man replies, 'I need to check with my supervisor. Can I place you on hold for one moment?'

'Of course,' I smile, picturing the young man sitting in a call centre somewhere in India next to his metal lunch box, layered with aloo paratha and pickles. And while I listen to the gentle jazz that temporarily takes his place, I play the conversation we'll have when he returns. How surprised he'll be when I disclose that I once lived in his country, when I tell him how I miss all my friends at the spice markets. I'll tell him that I still keep cardamom and cumin in my cupboard to remind me of those days. I could even tell him where I got the toe rings, or my silk curtains, which also came from Bombay. Mumbai. And wasn't it just a few minutes earlier when I was tying my wrappa that I was thinking how easy it was to tie a wrappa in comparison to the multiple folds of cloth needed for a sari. I'd always been useless with saris.

'Ma'am?'

'Yes.'

'Yes, that's quite fine, ma'am, I can add one more week.'

'Marvellous! Thank you,' I say, relieved. 'So tell me, sir, where are you calling from today? Is it bright and sunny?'

'Ma'am, I'm calling from Sacramento, ma'am. Yes ma'am I could say it's quite fine.'

'Oh,' I say, deflated. Sacramento was such a disappointing capital city. So lacking in character. No hills or mountains; just flat like a plate. What a shame he wasn't calling from India. And me, ready to exchange a few greetings in Hindi. Thank God I didn't embarrass myself. Still, there was something familiar sounding about his voice. I wonder if he's a former student? I miss my students. But if he was one of mine then why doesn't he recognize my name or voice?

'Okay ma'am,' he says, 'just to confirm, now your doctor has until the twelfth.'

'My doctor?'

'For the physical, ma'am.'

'Physical?' I glance again at the letter: the attached forms have to be completed by a doctor. Flipping through them, I see that in addition to the physical and mental-health test, an eye test is also required. 'Tell me, what's your name again? Sanjay? Is it customary for the DMV to send out these letters?'

'Actually, it's Sunil.'

I detect some impatience, but what does *he* have to be annoyed about?

'Actually,' he continues, 'we don't actually do this, ma'am. I mean, what I mean is that it comes from head office. So, like all I know is that this happens if someone reports you, for let's say, like actually careless, or, like reckless driving.'

'Careless?' I ask, because it's his syntax that merits the label 'careless' not my driving. 'Well, I'm sure that sometimes I've parked a little too far from the pavement and maybe occasionally too close to the pavement or 'kerb' as you may call it, but surely these are just minor mistakes?' I pause, waiting for him to laugh, and when he doesn't I continue undeterred. 'I suppose that once or twice my car might have stalled going up hill, but isn't that to be expected in San Francisco? You see my car is a manual one. It's an old manual car. It's actually a collector's item.' But by now I've concluded that he won't know what a 911 is, not to speak of my 993. He's probably one of those that dreams of owning a Lexus with gold-rimmed hubcaps.

'Yes ma'am, anything else I can do for you, ma'am?'

'No, darling,' I mumble. 'No,' I repeat, because now I'm annoyed at having slipped into using this endearment which was a mannerism I'd once vowed never to adopt. I saw how it aged a friend, even more than her smattering of silver hairs and varicose veins that she was so fond of bemoaning. Calling a young man 'darling' or 'sweetheart' made you sound old, but now I'd just done it myself, without even thinking. '*Chouchouter,*' I whisper, failing to find a suitable English word. Belatedly, hearing the dull hum on the telephone line, I realize that my young American darling has hung up. 'Fuck! Bugger!' I add, startled by the crassness of my own language. Not as bad as the saccharine I'd used earlier, but still, my father would be appalled if he could hear me now. I wave the letter to the heavens in a gesture of apology before folding it and placing it back on the desk.

'I'm not careless,' I mutter to my friends on the shelves. 'Whoever's done this nasty thing of reporting me ought to be ashamed.'

My new optician tells me there's nothing he can do to stop the slow deterioration of my eyesight; and because I'd passed my last driving test without anyone noticing how I'd had to squint or lean forward to read the eye chart, I presumed that I'd be fine. I reckoned I had at least five more years of driving. 'At *least* five,' I tell myself firmly, deciding to deal with the letter later and take my walk before the fog rolls in. No point in getting my knickers in a twist over this. I fetch my keys, close the front door and take the stairs down to the lobby. On my way out I glance ruefully at Buttercup, my beloved old Porsche, parked admittedly a little more than eighteen inches from the kerb. But what the hell!

2

Dawud is embarrassed at not knowing the woman's name especially when she remembers his and even speaks a little of his language, so he hands her a flower.

'*As-salaam alaikum*. Beautiful flower for a beautiful woman,' he says in anticipation of the pleasure his words will bring.

'*Bellissimo!*' she smiles, flirtatiously tucking it above her ear.

He chuckles, thinking that once upon a time she must have been stunning – such a tall woman with a fine ass, even now. She was probably even stylish, although now, at her age, all these bright colours with the pencil and flowers sticking out of her hair only made her look odd. And if she did buy something, which wasn't often because she was one of those that preferred the organic place down the street, then it was always their cheapest flowers or a small packet of apricots. And this never made sense to him because if she bought all that expensive stuff down the road, then why didn't she also buy his expensive flowers? Amirah said the woman was just eccentric, but that was his sister being kind. Amirah never said a bad word about anybody, which is why he had to look after the family's business, and that was a headache with the shop being so close to the Haight Ashbury with all the hippies and pot-smoking lazies.

'Hey,' he calls to a woman who has just arrived. 'Can I help you?' Not so much a question as a warning because he's heard from the gym down the road that there's an Asian couple going round, stealing phones – one to distract, the other to snatch. 'One dollar seventy-nine,' he says, ringing up the chocolate – one eye on the till and the other on the suspect.

The woman takes the change and drops it, all of it, into his box for Palestinian orphans.

'Thank you, honey,' he smiles. Okay, so maybe he misjudged? But more likely, the only reason she didn't steal was because she saw him paying attention. She was probably thinking that $3.21 made a good investment if it meant that next time he wouldn't pay attention. But he's not that stupid. You don't take a man uprooted from Jaffa and forced to walk with his family across the desert and expect him to know nothing. No. You can't fool a man like him. He knows what people are like, which is why his sister ought to listen when he tells her that a chain of falafel stores is what they should be doing. He knows these things. He senses them. They could make it here in San Francisco just like the French restaurants in Russian Hill, the Mexican restaurants in the Mission, or the Italian ones all over the place. Why not Palestinian? They could call it Jaffa, or Falafel Meister, or whatever sounded good to Amirah. It would be cheap, good, healthy, and even organic. Low fat, vegan, raw, paleo, whatever people wanted, they could do it – cheap, easy, fresh. And once they made it in San Francisco then Oakland and then to LA and then to New York. To everywhere! But instead, what did Amirah want? Who the hell was gonna buy cakes in this neighbourhood? Expensive cakes, forget it. Cheap cakes maybe. But expensive cakes, no way. Why? Because women in this country were always dieting, and real men, like real men everywhere, didn't eat cake. Falafel yes, but not cake. Maybe birthday cakes for kids. But even then, think about it, Amirah. One kid would want a train cake, then another the clown cake, and then another's gonna start crying for a cake in the shape of a ballerina. And who's gonna make those sort of cakes? Not Amirah. She wanted the fancy ones with honey and pistachios like back home, but the problem was that Americans don't like those cakes. Too many nuts. Nuts, he kept reminding her. It made no difference that this was the home of peanut butter. Americans had a problem with nuts, and God forbid that one day some kid decided to have an allergic reaction to one of Amirah's cakes, then what? Then the business would be finished, that's what. He shakes his head and sighs as he returns to the bucket of flowers where the African still stands.

'For you, honey,' he says, handing her a second cutting.

Dawud's flower, when I brought it to my nose, smelled strongly of his aftershave, and this was what reminded me of Walid. In the early 1950s, before I was sent away to an English boarding school, we lived close to a Lebanese family. None of the family's children went to my father's church, but a few attended the church school, one of which was Walid. He had bright green eyes, just like Dawud's, and whenever it was his turn to lead morning devotionals he would do so with gusto, reading always from the Song of Songs. So of course I fell in love, and because Walid conveniently lived next door it was easy for me to meet him after school without my parents knowing. Once, I accompanied him to the room in his house known as 'the men's room', with low couches and heavy carpets hanging from the walls. The older men eyed the two of us through puffs of cigarette smoke. No doubt they were wondering, as I would later, how it came to be that a young African girl, attached in some manner to one of their young pubescent sons, came to be in their midst listening to the sing-song of their Arabic language and breathing deeply from the mingle of sweet cologne and tobacco. Or perhaps they didn't care. Perhaps they took it for granted that one of theirs would sow his wild oats with a black girl. In any case, as for Dawud, he ought to understand that for all his sweet talk and pleasing scent, it takes much more than tired sprigs of lilac to impress me. Although I know, of course, that he's not really trying to impress me. He just thinks he's being charming to an old lady. And yet, had he seen me in my youth – even in my middle years, things would have been different. Back then he would have had to work hard to get my attention.

'Really, I remind you of someone?' Dawud smiles. He likes Nigerians and plays soccer with three of them on Sunday afternoons in Oakland, but Morayo's already moved on.

'You know it's my birthday soon,' he overhears her saying to his sister, to which he rolls his eyes because he could swear this woman had a birthday every six months.

'You tell me what you need,' he hears Amirah offering. 'I'll make you a cake. Anything you need, honey.'

'Anything you need,' Dawud mutters, shaking his head at his sister's naivety. He sighs while watching birthday woman walk back to the bucket of short-stemmed tulips, which aren't his cheapest flowers today, but not the most expensive either. The woman leans in as if to smell, but he knows her well enough to guess what she's really doing. She's inspecting, trying to decide the best value for her money. But then she surprises him by picking two bunches instead of one – one purple, one pink. She shakes off the excess water, takes them to Amirah, and pays.

'Organic!' He calls after her, winking when she catches his eye.

'*Shukran!*' she calls back.

3

I resume my walk down Stanyan Street, puzzling for a moment over Dawud's words. His jovial exterior doesn't fool me because I know he's led a hard life. He's been divorced, he suffers from back pain, and Amirah has told me that it was political trouble that caused their mother to send him out of Ramallah. I imagine him as an angry teenager, throwing stones at Israeli soldiers; but nothing more serious, for how else would they have given him refuge in America?

'You look awesome,' says a stranger, startling me from my thoughts.

'Well so do you,' I smile, noting the man's carefully manicured lime-green fingernails. I enjoy this sort of attention from San Francisco's gentlemen. It's one of the things that I love about the city. And because of men like this, men not sexually attracted to women, I find this city gentler than most. And what's more, here in San Francisco, both men and women seem to admire my sense of style. Whereas if I were back in London or certain parts of New York, where buba and gele are commonplace, I know that I wouldn't turn heads, not at this age at least. And back in Nigeria, where so many are dressed like me, I wouldn't draw any attention at all. So I treasure this city with its bright morning sun and brilliant blue skies. I love the way the fog rolls in late in the day, tumbling over Sutro Forest, to cloak my part of the city in soft white mist. But it's the people of San Francisco, so often quirky but always friendly, that makes it feel like home to me. And then I hear a car that roars the way mine does. Which reminds me. What the hell will I do if I don't pass the eye test? It's not the first time I've fretted over this, but previously I've always managed to talk myself out of worrying. I turn left now on Parnassus to sit for a moment at the bus stop and catch my breath. I perch on the edge of a red plastic seat, clutching the tulips tightly to my chest, considering my options – public transportation or a chauffeur. Is that really all there is? And public transport isn't as convenient as it is in London. I've had drivers in the past, but in a different context, different country. In San Francisco a driver will be expensive. And anyway, I want to remain independent – to be able to take off whenever I feel like it. It's not just a question of getting from A to B, but the freedom to do as I choose.

I must have walked several blocks before noticing the homeless man in front of me. Seeing how dejectedly he moves, it makes me feel selfish for having worried so much about the DMV. I drop back a step and watch as the man's dog follows, the leash trailing behind. I'm reminded of a summer in Lagos when an American preacher came to Nigeria and walked around carrying a cross on his back. It was the year that Caesar was in between his Delhi and Paris tours and just a few years into our marriage, when I discovered that Caesar had another wife. I was in such shock that I considered leaving Caesar that very day, picking up my own cross and following the preacher. I stare now at the back of this man's legs, muddied and clad in the remnants of blue jeans.

On the man's backpack is a tangle of straps and tags flapping angrily in the wind and when the puppy stops to squat I pass discretely in front of them both, keeping my distance in case of lice or some sudden outburst. I expect him to smell badly but he doesn't, and, glancing back, I see that he's actually a she and shockingly young to be carrying such a load. Seventeen or eighteen judging from the slenderness of the girl's arms; except that when I stop to look again and glimpse those steely, tiger-blue eyes, I'm no longer sure. She could be in her thirties, maybe even forties. I watch as the woman stops, reaches into a nearby trashcan, whips out some newspaper, and tears off a sheet before turning back to where the puppy's just been. She scoops up the steaming black pellets then chucks them in the trash. 'Come on, Stupid,' she mutters to the dog.

'You okay, love?' I ask.

'Yep,' she says, then turns at Fredrick Street and yells 'you fucker!' to a young man just arrived with skateboard in hand. A flurry of insults rain down on the poor man's head for having left her on her own to deal with the puppy and backpack. Startled, but then bemused and wishing I'd had more of the woman's spirit when I was younger, I say to the man in the car that has stopped for me at the zebra crossing, 'Did you hear that woman? Did you see how tough she was?' To which the driver only waves me on, but I've just looked up and spotted a stracciatella sky, dappled blue and white. 'Consider the birds in the sky,' my father used to say, 'that neither sow nor reap and yet your heavenly father feeds them.' So why worry about a driving licence? I ask myself.

'Cross the fucking street, would you lady!' shouts the man in the car.

The bakery on Cole Street is my favourite because of its walnut bread and the pain au raisin that's not too sticky, not too sweet and almost as good as the ones we used to buy in France when we lived on the *rue de* what-was-it-called in the 15th *arrondissement*. But it's not just the food that's good here: it's also the chance I have to chat with friends. Here, for example, is where I meet Alonzo and Mike who park in front of the fire hydrant where parking is not generally permitted. They swagger in, hands on hips, just like in the movies with baton, handcuffs and pistols swinging from their waists. They tuck their crackling radio devices into chest pockets while chatting to those in the cafe. I say Alonzo and Mike because they work as a team, but it's Mike that I'm closest to. He's writing a novel, you see, so we talk about books. When he's done with his first draft, I've promised to read it and give him feedback. He helped me, years ago, get out of a ticket for an alleged traffic offence. Bless him.

The incident happened at month-end, which, if you're familiar with San Francisco, is when the city goes on the prowl for extra money. This would explain why the cop who pulled me over was hiding round the corner, trying to catch people out for traffic violations. I thought I *had* come to a full stop at the four-way intersection, but I didn't argue. I wasn't as fearful as I would've been were I younger, but I still knew better than to court a policeman's anger when he repeatedly asked me if I was the owner of such an expensive car. I could tell he was suspicious, so I sat quietly as he wrote out the ticket. A few days later when I saw Mike, I recounted what had happened. 'Let me take care of it,' he offered. And he did. And at first I felt triumphant. It was like being back in Nigeria where, because I knew someone, I was able to work the system. Mike's parents came from Italy and I've always thought there is much that binds Italians with Nigerians. Not that I approve of corruption, but in this case, where I knew I'd done no wrong, I felt vindicated. And yet the following month when I went to the courts to hear that my case was dismissed, instead of feeling happy, I felt ashamed. So many young black men were at the courts – some of them going out of their way to give me a hand up the stairs. They even let me pass in front of them in the queue to get my papers. They gave me preferential treatment as they would their mother or grandmother and yet I didn't deserve it. I had connections. I had '*le piston*' to get me out of there, but they possessed no such social capital. They didn't have the means or the connections to wriggle out of paying fines as I had. Many, I could tell, were already stuck in the system and would never get out.

Mike isn't here today, but there's the white fellow who always wears Sikh turbans and silver bangles with one of his stupid birds on his shoulder. I'm sorry, but you'll have to forgive me. I cannot, as a good Nigerian, approve of such a thing. If Selvon's Sir Galahad had been around, I bet he would've eaten all of these birds for dinner. It's bad enough that the street pigeons feel free to waddle in through the cafe door and that the bird lovers won't shoo them out, even when they keep returning, greedily waddling back for seconds with their heads jerking to a cocky hip-hop beat. So that's bad enough, but this business of bringing birds into a restaurant on your arm or shoulder, well I really can't be dealing with that. No Nigerian would. Nor an Italian, I'm sure.

I'd come to the bakery to talk to my new friend, the cashier, but because she isn't here I buy some bread, linger for some minutes in case someone else arrives. When nobody does, I leave. I was hoping to invite my friend to the birthday party because I find that parties in which everyone is the same age aren't much fun. I can't have a party just for older people, and in any case, chronological age aside, I don't feel old. Or at least I didn't until I started noticing the absence of younger friends, which got worse once I stopped teaching. And that's another problem with this city. It's harder to make young friends here than it is in places like Lagos or Delhi. In San Francisco, people tend to stick to those of their own age set. And though I know that my friend, Sunshine, will come – one youngster won't be enough. I was also hoping to give my new friend some tulips, but now I suppose I'll have to keep both. I look around, thinking of the young homeless woman and then, for a moment, of Mrs Dalloway and her delphiniums. Mrs Dalloway chose stiff and stately flowers for her party whereas I've opted for tulips that arch and curve and keep growing after being cut. Fairly apt I'd say, on a day that started off with the DMV and all that jazz.

I take Cole Street home and on my way back I say hello to Mrs Wong who lives at the corner of Alma and Cole. At this time of year old Mrs Wong, dressed in bedroom slippers and pink dressing gown, spends much of the day sweeping leaves. Every few minutes the wind whips up new leaves and blows more off the trees. Mrs Wong's appearance is unfortunate – her terry cloth dressing gown and her hunched posture make her look much older than she probably is. I offer her my extra bunch of flowers which she accepts with effusive thanks, dropping her broom to hug the tulips and then me. I smile and draw back my shoulders. Nobody will ever call me a *little* old lady. When I get home, I punch in the code and push my way through the heavy front door, resting for a brief moment to catch my breath before climbing the stairs. There's a box on my doorstep filled with bright yellow Meyer lemons. 'Such a lovely man,' I smile for I know who this is. My neighbour from downstairs is persistent; I must give him credit for that. But he's a Republican and he owns a gun so he stands no chance with me. No chance. I balance the bread and the flowers on top of the box of lemons and then with my free hand I search for the keys in both pockets of my bra, only to find that the front door is already open. Forgetful me! I pick everything up, glance around to make sure nobody else is here, then carry the box to the kitchen table and select a lemon to rub between my fingers. I love the fresh smell of citrus so I place some in my white fruit bowl and take them to the living room where I set them on a shelf.

As you will see, I no longer organize my books alphabetically, or arrange them by colour of spine, which was what I used to do. Now the books are arranged according to which characters I believe ought to be talking to each other. That's why *Heart of Darkness* is next to *Le Regard du Roi,* and *Wide Sargasso Sea* sits directly above *Jane Eyre.* The latter used to sit next to each other but then I thought it best to redress the old colonial imbalance and give Rhys the upper hand – upper shelf. I turn from my books for a moment, distracted by a noise, but it's only the familiar thwack of tennis balls and the shudder of basketballs against backboards coming from the primary school across the street. Coming back to the bookshelf I pull out a book at random and a postcard falls out. It's one of his, of course. Fulani woman with bronze earrings. I flip it over again and trace each crafted line with my forefinger, then bring it to my nose and smile. '*Eu te amo.* Antonio,' he'd signed, with the arrow of the last 't' pointing achingly off the page. I sigh, trying to remember what he looked like. I remember his eyes, which were light brown. And his hands, I remember those. I remember the first time he touched me, taking my hand under cover of dark. We sat in the cinema watching Lord only knows what, for his thumb was tracing circles in the centre of my palm and it took all my concentration to stop from moaning out loud. He was always so gentle, except when he wasn't, which was sometimes even more thrilling. But it was his words above all else that drew me to him and his love letters, brimming with tenderness and desire.

I return to the kitchen and make myself some tea. Standing by the sink in *tadasana*, I gaze across the city, I think of Mrs Manstey in her solitary New York apartment. And then as the neighbour's washing machine thumps to the end of a spin cycle, I hear the noise again; only this time the sound is unmistakable. I'm surprised at first, not in the noticing of it but in the wave of desire that grips my body as I put down my green Harrods mug and step quietly out of the kitchen into the living room. The whimpering has grown louder, as does the quickening thud that gives rhythm to the couple's lovemaking in the apartment next door. I make my way to the couch where I lie on the futon, smiling as I sweep around my mind for a suitable person with whom to enjoy this unexpected surge of feeling. It's Dawud that joins me first, smelling of falafel and lilac as we lie together, legs intertwined. I kick a cushion out of the way and then it's the neighbour that takes Dawud's place, his calloused hands gently cupping my breasts as he massages my nipples. But soon, inevitably, it's Antonio whose fingers slip between my thighs, his breath tickling my neck. I close my eyes now as I whisper his name and then, letting go, I abandon him for the warmth that my touch has kindled. Only later, when I'm lying still, do I think again of Antonio and wish that he were here lying next to me. The two of us, pressed together. I bring my arm down from where I'm surprised to find it, flung above my head, and clasp my hands across my breasts. I must have then dozed for a little while because when I awake, everything around me is quiet. I get up, re-tie my wrappa and plump a cushion back into shape. I find my glasses on the kitchen counter and smile as I catch my reflection across the belly of my silver kettle. I peer closer, remembering how Antonio used to call my eyes his 'love crumbs'. Poetry, he told me, stolen from Cummings. As I wait for the water to boil, I remember some of our secrets and I miss him. But then I remind myself that perhaps it's less him and more the idea of him that I'm missing. How often I have felt lonely even when with someone. Lonelier sometimes than when I'm on my own. I lift the teabag out, squeeze it and plop it down on the saucer by the side of the kettle. Gently, like the touch of Antonio's thumb, I stir and stir until there's no more sugar at the bottom of my mug. 'Wanna little sugar in my bowl,' I hum, dancing playfully towards the bedroom to take another look at my new shoes.

This year the shoes are red and suede and although they're not cheap, or rather *because* they're not cheap, they're gorgeous. 'Absolutely gorgeous,' I whisper, freeing my hands in order to try them on. I have two traditions when it comes to birthdays. The first is to buy shoes, and this year's shoes have a sensible wedge heel with a peek-a-boo toe. On the outside they're a deep, plush scarlet red, and because it's a big birthday, I match the shoes with my black chiffon dress and double string of pearls. Pearls that have accompanied me to all manner of places – from lunch with Mrs Gandhi to tea at Buckingham Palace, to this little place where I really must get round to replacing the broken glass in my full-length mirror. I climb onto the ledge of the bath and hold firmly to the edge of the door to balance. This way I can see both the shoes and the dress in the bathroom mirror and imagine, right there, where I place the palm of my hand, the spot for a tattoo. For this is my second tradition, to do something new and daring with each passing year. Last year it was scuba diving, and the year before learning to swim. This year it's the tattoo and it's not just the fact of getting a tattoo but it's where I intend to have it done that thrills me. I'd decided that something on the wrist or ankle would be too ordinary and this was my reason for wanting to talk to my bakery friend. I was hoping to ask her what she thought of bougainvillea – of a long fine thread of it winding its way up my back. Was that a good idea? It was also the reason for purchasing tulips in two different colours, wanting to know which shade she'd recommend or whether she'd suggest no colour at all – just the regular black. Was it black or dark green that most tattoos came in these days? And what colour would look best on my darker skin? My bakery friend has a Chinese dragon that spreads across her back with its feet perched on her thigh. She showed it to me unprompted one day, and explained how it represented her family's heritage. She said she'd had it done in three sittings to manage the pain. I wonder how long it will take to do my flowers. Not long, I hope, because I don't like needles. I cringe at the thought of all those childhood vaccinations for nasty diseases. Tetanus. Typhoid. Diphtheria. Yellow Fever. I wonder now if it might be better to choose a design that's smaller. Perhaps I should just have a small sprig of bougainvillea – something like the size of one of Dawud's gifts – inked at the base of my neck. I'd never have the courage for something as big as a dragon, but perhaps I could have a tiny little blossom, symbolic of the tropical climes that I so love. Yes, I'm beginning to think that this is a good idea. What could be more perfect to mark my seventy-fifth than this? I twist for a better view and then, in mid-twist, I slip.

4

'You're lucky, ' says the Activities Director at the Good Life Rehabilitation Center.

'Yes,' I nod, because I know I'm lucky that a neighbour was at home to hear me fall. And I know that my injuries could have been worse, much worse. And were I not in pain I might have responded more cheerfully; instead I take a deep breath, willing my body into stillness and calm. But today my body wants nothing to do with its old yogi self. I'm feeling exhausted and don't like the fact that someone has dressed me in a loose fitting T-shirt without a bra. And I don't like the fact that this sweetly perfumed woman is sure to notice my sour morning breath. So I abandon my deep *anahata* breathing and turn my head, looking to the tabletop for painkillers.

'What can I get you?' the woman offers.

'Nothing, I'm fine,' I say, because now that I've found my glasses, I can see that she's not that much younger than me. 'I just don't like feeling so disorientated.'

'It's because of the drugs, hon, still working their way out of your system. You must try to rest.' She squeezes my hand gently.

'Maybe I just need something to take my mind off it.' I prop myself up so as not to be in such a helpless position.

'Whenever you're ready,' she says, 'we've got lots of activities. We've got ragtime music, which is happening as we speak, knitting circle and sewing circle ... There's even speed walking, hula hooping, and the iPad 101, which we've just added.'

'Books are what I'd really love.' I answer, wriggling my hand free.

'Have you seen the library?'

'No,' I say. The books that I want are my own books, but the woman has already started to enthuse about the library. She proudly lists some authors who've come to speak as if I should have heard of them, but I don't recognize any of the names. I suspect that none have great literary merit. Then the woman's phone rings and she apologizes for having to leave. I, on the other hand, am relieved. Now that she's gone, I reach across the bedside table for the one book that I do have and slump back into bed. I know I'm lucky, I know I am, but I don't like being this fragile and feeling this out of control.

I'd packed the book in my earthquake kit years ago and then forgotten about both, but whoever found me after the fall must have discovered the bag next to the bed and thought it was my regular handbag. Funny how this emergency bag had come with me even though it wasn't the sort of emergency I'd been planning for. Earthquakes and tsunamis were what I'd expected. But wasn't that the thing about life? It was always the unexpected, those events not planned for, that got you in the end. I'd never much liked the feel or smell of this snakeskin bag but I'd kept it for nostalgia's sake. An elderly Hausa trader had sold it to me in Kano and because I'd bought it at the market with my mother, and because the trader insisted that it would bring me good luck, I'd never got rid of it. The good luck I'd hoped for as a child was for God to cure me of my nearsightedness. I'd once read about a girl who'd lost her glasses, prayed for them to be found, only to be surprised when God answered her prayers by curing her eyesight. So this was the sort of miracle that I'd been hoping for. I'd even taken to rubbing the bag like an Aladdin's lamp until it dawned on me that God might disapprove. Rubbing lamps in hope of magic wasn't exactly the Christian thing to do. I'd probably jinxed my chances. But perhaps, after all these decades, this might now be the good luck moment that the trader had foretold, for there's nothing else in the room to keep me occupied – a bed, chair, commode, a dresser with TV, and a tray of African violets on the windowsill. The little mauve flowers sit in a shallow plastic tray that might once have been someone's lunch tray. And now that the pain is subsiding I close my eyes and focus on my breath. I'm breathing in, breathing out. What a dreadful list of activities on offer at this place.

I drift to sleep and imagine skydiving and belly dancing. And then I'm dreaming of racing cars at the Safari Rally where Buttercup and I speed towards the finishing line in a plume of red dust.

I awake to the sound of voices coming from outside. Spanish speaking. Someone mentions a party and then there's laughter. I'm irritated by how much noise they're making as I try shifting my torso for a less painful position. I cough to clear my throat then reach across the bedside table feeling around for a glass of water. My hand finds my glasses and the book instead, so I take them and try cheering myself with thoughts of home and the books awaiting my return. I keep the books that used to belong to my mother in my bedroom. All her Beatrix Potters are in the tiny shelves behind the glass doors of the cabinet. The dictionaries and magazines sit at the bottom and everything else lives in between. Caesar wouldn't have approved. He would've said the place was too cluttered.

I was twenty-two when we were married, and Caesar thirty-seven. Caesar was younger than my father, but not by much. He had my father's confidence and self-assuredness but, unlike father, Caesar was world-travelled and university educated which meant he spoke with scholarly knowledge (not just personal conviction) on what was best for Nigeria, what was best for our continent. I was proud of the way people listened to Caesar – of the way people leant forward so as not to miss a single word he said. Caesar spoke quietly, almost inaudibly at times, which was one of the characteristics that initially drew me to him; but over time this mannerism lost its allure and I began to see it as nothing more than practiced charm. I lost faith in politics and grew impatient with those clinging to my husband's every word, with the women especially, who flattered him, making him think he could and should become Nigeria's next president.

Antonio was initially Caesar's friend. He had come to Nigeria as Brazil's first black cultural ambassador. He was a photographer and soon beloved by the Lagos elite as much as by those on the streets and villages that he most enjoyed photographing. He was younger than me by several years and a follower of the Candomblé religion – two more reasons (in addition to him being Caesar's friend) why I didn't expect to fall for someone like him. But then I also hadn't expected to be married to someone already married. In the end it was Antonio rather than the preacher that I went running to when I learned about Caesar's first wife. Antonio was the man who always had time for me, the man for whom pomp and ceremony meant nothing, and the man who asked questions that had nothing to do with the perfunctory. The man that took photographs and believed in the power of art, that believed art could change the world. It was enough sometimes for me just to recall the touch of Antonio's hand brushing against mine to feel aroused, and then to fantasize about what it might feel like to do more. I imagined many forbidden acts, many places where we might travel together, where we'd dance, laugh, and make love. I imagined being fearless even while wrestling with the fear of betraying my husband (in spite of his betrayal of me) and the fear of being shamed in front of all our friends and in front of Antonio's sweet wife. Most of all, I feared disappointing my father who'd suffered enough shame with my mother's death.

5

The message gives no details beyond Morayo's name: nothing about how or when and only that such-and-such a number could be called for more information. It takes me some time to find anyone who knows about the case, but eventually a nurse confirms that Morayo is indeed in hospital, that she's had a fall and is undergoing hip surgery. Shocked, I recall my many promises to have tea with her and bring the boys. Every week there'd been some new excuse and I hadn't gone.

St Mary's Hospital isn't far from the boys' school so the following morning, after dropping the children off, I buy flowers and drive there. I hadn't checked the visiting hours but decided, if anyone questioned me, I'd just say I was Morayo's daughter. I'm sure this is how Morayo would have described me to the hospital staff anyway, 'Sunshine, my daughter.' So I take the elevator to the seventh floor, pleased when nobody stops me. The area around Morayo's bed is cordoned off from neighbours by a plastic floral curtain and I find her on her back, breathing through her mouth. Gently, I place my hand on her wrist and whisper hello. A few stiff white hairs sprout from her otherwise dark eyebrows. I'm sad to see her looking so tired, and older than the last time I'd seen her. I pat her hand and whisper that I'll be back. I need to put the flowers in water. There's a side table but no vases. I should have thought of this before.

They're busy at the nurses' station but after a few minutes someone offers to help, and after several more minutes of scrabbling around I'm given a plastic water cup. It's inelegant and too small, but I do my best to make Morayo's favourite flowers stand up straight while the same nurse now attends to her.

'Hello Mrs Da Silva,' the nurse repeats. 'How are you feeling? Sleepy? You have a visitor.' Then turning to me, 'It's the drugs, you know, that cause the drowsiness. Mrs Da Silva?' She keeps calling until Morayo opens her eyes, squints at the nurse and then at me.

'Hi,' Morayo whispers, a smile of recognition lighting her face. She tries lifting her hand from the cover then drops it when she sees the intravenous drip attached to the back of her hand.

'I'm so glad you're okay,' I stroke her arm.

'Sunshine?'

'Yes,' I smile.

'Is every, every?'

'Everything's fine,' I say, sensing her struggle with the words.

'She'll be tired for the next few days,' explains the nurse, as Morayo's eyes flutter for a moment then close again. 'She'll do rehab, then physical therapy. The good thing is that recovery from hip surgery is usually quick. It's what happens afterwards that you gotta keep an eye on, honey. Gotta keep her moving. You don't want blood clots. She's gotta get those muscles strong again. You don't want repeat falls, that's the danger to watch for.'

I'm careful not to touch anything as I leave the hospital. I press the buttons of the elevator with my elbow and as soon as I step out, I pull out a hand sanitizer, meticulously wiping my fingers and then the length of my arms, before disposing of the wipe. I do it again, just to be sure, before checking my phone for any new messages.

I know Morayo's building well. Ten years ago I used to live there and that's when we first met – one emotion-filled afternoon. My in-laws had been staying, and the strain of having to be the dutiful, doting daughter-in-law in a too-small apartment, with Zach still in diapers and Avi a colicky newborn, had proven too much for me. I'd fled to the laundry room trying to pull myself together, but as soon as Morayo asked what was wrong I'd burst into tears. As sometimes happens with the unexpected kindness of strangers, I found myself telling her everything. I told her how inadequate I was feeling, for it seemed that no matter how hard I tried I would never be good enough for my in-laws: never lady-like enough, never subservient enough, never educated enough, but most of all, never "Indian enough". It was the latter that bothered me the most until Morayo reassured me by saying, 'There's no such thing, darling, as being "Indian enough", no such thing as one Indian culture.' And because she was the same age as my in-laws and because she'd lived in India as well as in Africa, I trusted her.

When I arrive at Morayo's apartment and open her front door I'm surprised to find how hot and musty it is and how cluttered. 'My God,' I mutter, looking around at all the books and papers. When was I last here? Surely not that long ago? Books are everywhere, strewn haphazardly across the shelves, some with spines facing inward, others facing out. Nothing on the shelves is arranged alphabetically, even though several months earlier the two of us had spent a whole day alphabetizing her books. Now, like abandoned children's toys, I discover many more books tucked away in clothes drawers and cupboards. Nothing seems to be in order, and if I didn't know Morayo better, I might have wondered at the state of her mind. But nothing's wrong with Morayo. Or is there? Papers and unopened bills are piled on the table. How would I find time to clear it all up? I'd have to hire someone, but there's no time for that now either. All I can do today is make sure the lights are switched off, check that there's nothing that needs to be thrown out in the fridge, and find a few books to take on my next visit. 'But which books, for Christ's sake?' In her bedroom I find two newer-looking ones, including a memoir by Maya Angelou. At least I've heard of her. Morayo is always giving me books to read but most I find to be too dense, which is why I'm pleasantly surprised to discover a stack of glossy romance books next to her bed. 'Not what I would have expected from you, Professor Morayo,' I laugh to myself. But then again, perhaps I shouldn't be surprised. Morayo was so uninhibited, so open and unconventional in comparison to most old people. There couldn't be many women of her age who would choose to spend their savings on a beautiful sports car. I go to the kitchen, pour out the dregs of several accumulated mugs of tea and wipe down the surfaces. I'm almost ready to leave when I hear a rustle. I turn, and then scream when I see what's perched on the stove. By the time someone comes, the mouse has long gone. Disappeared behind the oven to meet what I imagine must be a multitude of brothers and sisters.

I call Francisco, the man who helps me with odd jobs. Two days later I leave him in Morayo's apartment to sort through things and when I return, the home is beautifully transformed. Surfaces are cleared and books are standing upright on the shelves. The larger books that don't fit on the shelves are stacked in piles – duplicates in one pile, exactly as I'd requested.

'And the mouse?'

'Gone,' Francisco declares. 'Gone. But let me tell you something, this woman, I think she's keeping money everywhere. I find it in the books; I find it in the kitchen. It's everywhere, you know, like maybe she's too scared to go to the bank or something. I don't know, but here, look ...'

He hands me a stack of dollar bills; everything from one-dollar bills to a hundred, and several of those too.

'Maybe you need to tell her not to put money in all these places.'

'I will,' I nod, 'Thank you. And the other books?'

'The torn ones? Those ones, I threw them away.'

'You what?' I gasp. 'But, I didn't ask you to do that. I said the old newspapers and magazines. Not the books.'

'You said to me to throw all the torn stuffs away.'

'But no, that's not ...' I pause. I want to say *you must have misheard,* but I see from Francisco's aggrieved look that this will make things worse. The last thing I want is for him to feel offended by me saying his English isn't good. He's always complaining about people who are prejudiced against 'Latin people' and I don't want him treating me like just another racist gringo. 'Okay,' I manage, 'but now we've got to get the books back.'

'You want me to look in the garbage? It's a big garbage.' He says, raising an eyebrow.

By the time I get to the basement where the garbage bins are kept, I can't see the books. Whatever Francisco had thrown away is now buried beneath other people's trash – pizza and cereal boxes, glass bottles and soda cans and plastics. So much plastic! I briefly consider emptying the bin on the floor and sorting through it. Madness. By now the books would only be more ruined. So I tell myself that maybe this isn't as disastrous as it seems. Maybe most of those books should have been thrown out anyway. Morayo has so many books, too many books, more than she has room for. So

I leave the basement and the following day, the bins have been emptied.

6

'Okay, so the other day this black lady comes up to me. And I don't mean that in a bad way. I'm just saying, she was black. And tall and old. Not old-old, but definitely older than me: old enough to be my mom, maybe even my grandma. So anyway, she sees that I'm carrying all this shit, plus I had the dog so I guess she kinda felt sorry for me and then she kinda like asked me if I was okay. But sometimes you get tired of people looking at you like you need pity and shit like that. Yeah, I'm homeless! But so what? Maybe that's what I shoulda said, but the words don't always come out when you want them to.

Homeless is just because we're house challenged. We don't have a roof over our heads, but we make it work. Thank God I'm in the food industry and we have food. And I feel like I've learned a lot from living like this because you never starve, you're always clothed, you ground score everything, I mean basically. We help each other, you know. I go to people's parks a lot and I see a lot of it there. No one's better or different than the other person. We're all of one heart. We all care for each other. We have off days and on days just like everybody else does. I don't drink or anything like that, and I don't do drugs or anything like that anymore, and that's my choice. It's a perspective and a focus that I have to respect myself. And living like this, you can't live like this if you're high all the time. You can't. Or you'd lose focus and you'd be tired all the time. I have my car, and my dog and my stuff, and I have a job so I'm okay. And I've been married, I lived in Portland, lived in Oakland and Berkeley and had a really good childhood and stuff. My father made a lot of money back in the day for living in the Bronx. What people make today, my father made back then. Those kind of figures, you know. So I come from good stock. My dad was a saver, while I'm not. I'm a free spirit, you know, an artist.

I come from a family of artists and piano playing and music and stuff like that. We had a piano growing up in our house, in my grandmother's house when I was a kid. Ukuleles and mandolins and singing and dancing. You know, that's where I come from. That kinda of background. So that's how come the Grateful Dead really gave me that free spirit of danceability. I took modern dance. I had a recital at Carnegie Hall. I'm not saying that I'm a poor little rich girl or anything, but I come from good stock. And sure, I have a higher sight for myself, of course! But then I would wanna take everybody into my home, you know, and let them just have a good night's sleep, you know. Cos I know what it's like. And I haven't slept in a bed for three years, you know. But that's a journey in life, you know, it's like a journalist going to another country.

Like on a mission, like a missionary. And it's not that I don't sleep. I have a pillow and a comforter, you know. Down comforter. I had a sleeping bag. I gave that away. It's so good to give.

Giving! I've learned so much about just giving. Giving is such a good feeling. Buying someone a cup of coffee, or paying someone's toll, or someone doing that for me, you know. That act of kindness is A-MAY-ZING. Amazing! Be kind. It's very amazing. Sometimes we just don't take the time to know people as people and maybe someone's heart is broken in some way or another, you know.

So. Just to back-pedal back to that woman I was talking about earlier. Well, maybe her heart was broken, you know, and I shouldn't have been so like, 'I don't wanna talk to you.' You just never know. Be kind. Be kind. That's my new motto.

So like the other day, I found all these books just dumped onto the sidewalk. So I picked them up and I gave some to friends, who like to read, you know. But I kept one for myself cos there was one about Africa and I've always had this theory that Africans were the first to come to the Americas and that maybe some of my foremothers were African. So that's why I kept the book with Africa in its title, and I like the name on the inside page. Morayo Da Silva. I don't know how you pronounce it, but I kinda like More-RAY-oh cos it sounds like a ray of sunlight, genderless and grounded, just like my chosen name. Born Sarah, now Sage. And I'm still imagining my African ancestors coming up through Europe, across the Bering Strait, then down to the West Coast into the land of my other ancestors – the Cherokee tribe of the southeast and the Apache from the southwest. I also imagine that one day I'll dump my crazy ass boyfriend, let him take the dog, and then I'll go back to college and finish my degree, you know. That way I'll make something better for myself. I'll travel to Brazil. Maybe to Africa, cos when you think about it, really, with what I'm suffering now, my life isn't that much better than what Africans are living through, you know. I mean my life is okay and stuff, but I'm not gonna lie to you. It's tough out here, and sometimes when I read about Africa, I don't see America being any better. It's really a crying shame. A crying shame.

7

Sunshine tells me over the phone that it's only been three days, but it feels like it's been longer. I wonder if she's rounding down the number, trying to make me feel better. I just want to be back home.

Nights are the hardest, when I hear the neighbours having nightmares and the nurses bustling in their loose cotton trousers and rubber-soled shoes. I try blocking my ears to the screams, but that doesn't help much and I'm always startled when the pipes in my room begin to creak and wheeze. Sometimes I have nightmares of my own. I dream that someone's attacking me, and when I scream for help, no sound comes out. I awake, suffocating and gasping for breath. They've given me a panic button, supposedly for things like this, but I don't know who'll come if I press it, so I don't use it. I only wish they'd let me lock my door. Better still, that I were strong enough to push some heavy furniture against it. I know I ought to be safe here but I also know that you can never be sure.

There's a very nice woman called Bella and I wish she worked nights. It would make me feel safer if she did, but because she doesn't, I stay alert through the darkness. I think of all my friends in the city and others around the world who don't know I'm here. I don't want people visiting me in this place. It feels too depressing, which is why I've only told Sunshine. So I wait for the blue of night to fade into dawn, and only then, when the warm smell of maple syrup slips through the gap at the bottom of my door, do I let myself rest.

To comfort myself and stop my mind going round and round in circles, I close my eyes and inhale deeply, summoning the smell of moin-moin and akara. 'Or porridge might be nice,' I whisper to myself, reimagining Goldilocks as Afrolocks, just before Bella arrives with the pancakes and their accompaniments – miniature packets of grape jelly and pats of butter so cold they sit, like hard-boiled sweets, refusing to melt on the hill of pancakes.

'Mind the gap,' I repeat, wishing for the doors to slide open.

I think sometimes that I'm losing my memory. I'm more forgetful these days, and lying in bed all day, I worry. Will I become just another old woman with Alzheimer's? And who will look after me? As a child I only remember one mad person – man or woman, I forget. Was it a bare-breasted woman who removed her wrappa to reveal a torn and dirty petticoat? Did she shriek and scratch her head? Or does this memory come from the book of my imagination? Or was it a man with thick, knotty, lice-infested hair? He was the only bearded man I saw in those days. I never dared to look too closely for fear that his curses might land on me. All the children knew that somewhere between this madman's legs hung a large penis. Swinging. Menacingly.

At lunchtime and dinner, it's the smell of boiled potatoes that first fills the air here. It reminds me of my boarding school days where cod and boiled potatoes were served on Fridays. Shepherd's pie on Saturdays, and roast lamb and boiled potatoes on Sundays. All followed by wobbly Bird's custard or Rowntree's jelly. I don't think mother ever cooked potatoes. She used to cook rice – sifting it carefully before she boiled it, letting me run my fingers through the tray of white pearls in search of small brown stones that needed to be discarded. I remember that the rice came from India and sat in a huge white sisal bag in a dark pantry with the serving calabash resting on top. It was only from boarding school then that I remembered the smell of boiling potatoes along with the forlorn cry of Eastbourne's seagulls, and the matching greyness of its skies and pebble beaches. Now it feels not unlike those lonely evenings lying face up in my school bunk bed, crying because my mother had died and my father was so far away.

On my first night they wheeled me into the dining hall, but I haven't been back since. I keep remembering the man who repeatedly lifted an empty fork from his plate to his toothless mouth. One of the aides would sometimes come to his rescue, but as soon as the aide left to help someone else, he returned to shovelling air between his gums. I've named the poor man, Santiago. The one who tries not to think, only to endure. That's why I find it better to stay in my room, in the company of my own thoughts with my one book of poetry, delighting in Satin-Legs Smith.

8

I had planned, after retiring from the university, to try my hand at writing, starting with a novel set in Nigeria. This doesn't fall into my birthday bucket list of new and daring things to do. But perhaps it should do as I've found the writing to be much more challenging than expected. I named my main character Joslyn: a reference to my home city of Jos, as well as to my closest childhood friend, Jocelyn, the houseboy's daughter. I'd always hoped that Jocelyn would marry a kind man, give birth to healthy children, and lead a happy life; but we'd lost touch after I left for boarding school so I never knew what happened to her. The book would therefore be the story of a life imagined and hoped for. It would be a love letter, both to my friend and to Jos where the two of us had grown up. Though I'd returned to Lagos many times since my childhood, I'd only been back to Jos once and never since the troubles broke out between Christians and Muslims and never since the arrival of Boko Haram. I'd always hoped to return with father, but when he died I couldn't bring myself to go back. One morning, as I stood in my San Francisco kitchen drinking coffee, I opened my newspaper to find on the cover an aerial shot showing bodies in Jos, wrapped in brightly coloured Ankara prints. From a distance, they looked almost beautiful, scattered like crayons in a jumbo-sized box; until I read the headline and peered closer and saw that some of the bodies were splattered, and many soaked, in a deeper red not belonging to the original fabric. The accompanying text detailed the massacre. I doubted it was my Jocelyn, but what if it was? Her name was written right there in the article, bearing witness to how people fled in terror, climbing trees to get away. People ought to have been safe up in the mango trees behind the thick canopy of green leaves where we used to hide as children. But no, according to this Jocelyn, these mad people had chased them even there, before smoking them out – some burning, as they fell from the branches. The date was 11 September 2001.

I started sending money back home, to the orphans, even though I couldn't always be sure whether the money would reach those most affected. It felt better to be doing something rather than nothing. For how was it possible that this had happened in my home city – the place where I'd grown up and that I'd once described as the warmest, most generous place on earth, where parents routinely took it upon themselves to look after everyone else's children or discipline them if need be; the place where one always cooked for more than the number of people in one's household in case others dropped by;

the place where old people were never relegated to stuffy barracks to sit for hours waiting for death; the place where vegetable sellers routinely gave their loyal customers a *dash* of several guavas or a small calabash of tomatoes for the evening stew, something small for free; the place where people said 'sorry' whenever someone tripped or fell or grazed themselves because that was the linguistic mirror of a culture based on empathy, having nothing to do with who was at fault; the place where Muslims celebrated Christmas and Christians broke the fast during Ramadan with their Muslim brothers and sisters; the place where grown men held hands and grown women walked arm in arm; the place where the term 'cousin' was never used because all cousins were brothers or sisters; the place where Sundays were spent visiting friends and relatives; the place where weddings and funerals and naming ceremonies and baptisms and graduations and independence celebrations and governor's parties were lavish and celebratory; the place where everyone knew your family; the place where the type of atrocities you read about in history class concerning the Germans, the Russians, the Japanese, the Chinese, the Nicaraguans, the Boers and all those foreign people, was never supposed to happen to you, or to your loved ones. Ever. Until one day it did. And worse.

And because Joslyn no longer seemed fictitious, because the good life I'd dreamt of for Jocelyn and her children now felt so tenuous, I put the manuscript away on the highest shelf where I prayed that my character would be hidden, far from danger. I returned to the company of old literary friends and the characters that I had taught to so many students over the years. I went first to *Blindness* and

July's People, because if anyone could survive it would be the doctor's wife and Maureen. And then I found myself sketching new chapters in my journal and changing the endings of stories so that some of those female characters not allowed to make it in their original version did in mine. Mrs Manstey didn't die in a fire, Firdaus wasn't executed, and Magda never went mad. Ophelia didn't go mad. Diouna didn't go mad. Tess didn't go mad. Nor did Jane Eyre or Antoinette Cosway. And once I'd breathed new life into a story I was satisfied, until my next visit – at which point I might add a chapter or lift a character and take her to another book. It frustrated me though not to have finished Joslyn's story. What I needed was a generous soul, a character that could transform things, really transform things. So now, lying in bed with nothing better to do, I find myself casting around for additional characters. I think of how I'd like to revisit those that I hadn't read for some time. What if Magda had been able to pass her baby, safely, into the hands of a kind German woman? Thrust the baby into a stranger's arms who would then raise the young girl with love as someone might have done for any of Joslyn's children. Thinking of this makes me even more impatient to leave, to get back to those thick pencil marks made as a young student and the thin ticks added in later years to see what additional characters and plots I might weave into my story.

I wish I'd packed more than one book. I reach again for my earthquake bag, just to double check because it feels heavy enough to contain another book. Or two? If not, then what in the world was making this thing so heavy? Water. I'd have to remember next time not to bother with so much water. And what else? I feel something bulky in the inside zip and, just as I pull it out, I remember. Hidden in the side pocket are two sanitary pads, extra long with wings, and tucked into these are my British passport and some hundred-dollar bills. 'What luck,' I laugh. 'Remember this, Morayo. One passport. One thousand five hundred dollars.' And if indeed there were any bleeding limbs, then what better thing to staunch the flow of blood than a woman's sanitary pad?

9

I remember seeing Morayo on previous occasions, walking in Cole Valley. We'd never spoken but we'd nodded to each other, black person to black person. I'd always assumed she was African American until I overheard her speaking, and then, judging from the vaguely British-sounding accent, I wondered if she too came from the Caribbean. Originally. She certainly had class, which was immediately noticeable in her mannerisms and dress. Once I saw her sitting alone in one of the neighbourhood cafes with a cup of tea, an almond croissant and a book. I imagined a waiter arriving with a plate of smoked salmon, truffles and caviar. Not that the French cafe on Cole Street had such fancy dishes, but her sitting there, so tall and poised, made anything seem possible. So what a surprise, but also a shock, to find her several months later, here in the Home looking quite ordinary in plain slacks and baggy

T-shirt. There are some people in life that one just never expects to see in a place like this, doing physical therapy.

'Reggie Bailey,' I introduce myself, as we pass each other in the hallway.

'Morayo Da Silva,' she replies. 'Pleasure to meet you.'

'Pleasure to meet you too – Morayo, if I may?' I would like to ask her how she's doing. If there's anything I can do for her. But her trainer is waiting and I've never liked this man who thinks he has an incredible physique when in fact he doesn't. So I step politely around them and move on to where I will wait until my wife is ready.

I usually try to arrive at the Home in time to have breakfast with Pearl and stay for the day. I then leave after dinner, taking the bus to and from our house. It's less expensive this way and I don't have to worry about parking. I'm here almost every day, but I still feel guilty. The nurses tell me there's no need. They say it's easier sometimes when I'm not around, which I know is true, at least when Pearl is being washed, but that doesn't stop me from feeling badly. For months I'd managed to look after her by myself and when it was just the two of us she didn't make a fuss. I know of course that there's no pattern to the disease, no rationality to the jagged paths it scissors through my wife's brain, yet this doesn't stop me wishing for logical explanations. And though on her more lucid days Pearl used to insist that I start another life without her, and just remember the good times, this wasn't something I could ever do. If I'd been her, I wouldn't have wanted to be left alone. And I know that if she were the sort of person to say what she really wanted, instead of always thinking first about others, she would have wanted me to stay.

I sit in the garden while they give Pearl her bath. Shortly, once it's all done, I'll return. She'll be clean and have no memory of the bath. But for now I wait in the sun, on the bench, facing the main entrance. People come and go, buzzed in and out by the receptionist, who sits with her back to the outside world filing her nails and texting. All day long she's on that phone. All day long. She'll do well in old age, doing exactly as she's doing now.

There's a back entrance for deliveries, but this is the main scenic entrance for visitors and doctors. Sometimes, when watching new arrivals, I'm tempted to point out how poorly the Home is designed. I'd like to dissuade people from coming, especially if they appear mean or crotchety, for Pearl's sake. There are enough of these sorts already and fewer of the kindly ones. I think of Morayo and wonder if she's married. I wonder who visits her here. I've seen her with children. Grandchildren?

I check my watch. Quarter to ten. Now they'll have finished with Pearl's bath. They'll use two white towels to dry her and then they'll dress her and brush her hair. They'll sit her down and dab powder onto her face, then rouge, in two slanted rectangular blocks along the cheekbones, or what used to be cheekbones where now there is more skin than bone. Then they'll let her choose a lipstick and chuckle while they paint it on, for Pearl likes to smack her lips, making it tricky. Pearl will smile when they hold the mirror up for her to admire their work. I always tell Pearl how beautiful she looks after her bath, which is a compliment to her as much as to the nurses who smile so encouragingly while I struggle not to curse. Or cry. But for now the sun warms my skin so I stay some extra minutes. I squeeze the tennis ball that I always bring with me. If I had three I might try juggling, but with one I only squeeze then release, squeeze then release.

Looking across at the flower beds I wonder why they didn't build a tennis court or, at the very least, install a table-tennis table in place of all the flowers. The architects must only have thought of women when they designed retirement homes, and assumed they liked to sit and stare solemnly at gardens all day. Pearl preferred tennis to gardening, which was why our garden was always a practical one, filled with vegetables and herbs for cooking, rather than flowers. I can see Pearl now in her short pleated white skirt. I see her anticipating my serve, rocking back and forth like Billie Jean King, exaggerating to make me laugh, to distract me. I was always the better player but she was the smarter player, the smarter everything, and with tennis her strategy was to keep going until she'd exhausted me. I chuckle and shake my head.

Pearl never used to wear cosmetics – only a sliver of eyeliner on occasion, but never lipstick, nor rouge. She was beautiful without it. Often I find an occasion to wipe off the bright lipstick and rouge that the nurses like on her. It's a strange negative intimacy, but our only one these days apart from when we're sitting, holding hands, like one of the sad old couples featured in the Home's glossy brochure.

I can't pretend that I've never hoped Pearl might die, and not just for her sake. I dream of being held. Of being touched. Of being desired again. Of being recognized. Of not having to worry about what other people might one day think of this, might already be thinking. I fear that one day they'll say I must stop touching her when there's no way of knowing if I have her consent. I'm also afraid of the day when I'll stop wanting to touch her in this way. Afraid because that day has long since come and gone. I squeeze the tennis ball, tighter and tighter, before letting go.

10

The boys have gone to bed and Ashok and I return to work. This is the way it is on weekday nights in our household. Ashok sits behind his computer at the kitchen table, checking legal documents and sending emails, while I move about tidying up. Thankfully, tonight there are plenty of leftovers. Saves me from making sandwiches for the boys' lunch. I divide the pasta equally between two Tupperware boxes and sprinkle each with Parmesan – slightly more for Zach and less for Avi, my picky one. Then I admire my creation – wholewheat fusilli speckled pink and green with pancetta and zucchini. I'm good at this and still consider turning my culinary skills into a business. But yoga is what most excites me these days even though, of all my entrepreneurial ideas, it's the least liked by Ashok and his family. While Ashok says I can do whatever I want, I know what he'd prefer. Status matters to him, so while he'd happily boast about his Sunshine doing a graduate degree he wouldn't do the same for a teaching qualification. Not for yoga at least. Which is ironic given that yoga brings me closer to India, but I suppose not in the way that his high-class family desires. I reach for the box of cherry tomatoes, cut a few in half and wedge them, artistically, on top. *Snap, snap*, and there, lunch is done. Into the fridge they go with a Pink Lady apple on top of each.

'Chocolate?'

I take the bar from Ashok, break off a square then give the rest back. His shoulders are hunched so I massage them and then nuzzle the back of his neck. Aroused, he pushes his laptop away, pulling me round for a proper kiss.

'Don't go,' he pleads, his arm tightening around my waist.

'I'm not going,' I whisper, 'it's just that ...'

He frowns as I wriggle free.

'I'm trying to help Morayo with all of these papers,' I explain as I spread them across the kitchen table. Ashok nods, but I know he's disappointed. I wonder if I should explain that it's not that I don't want to make love, only that after a long day of attending to others I'm craving space. And even if it means that I continue to look after others, at least it's my choice rather than one of my duties as a mother. But we've had this conversation before so I stick to Morayo. 'Have you ever heard of the Abdul Rahim Centre for Rights to Education? I can't find anything about it online and I'm worried because Morayo seems to have sent them quite a lot of money.'

'Sounds like a scam to me,' he mutters.

'But just because we can't find anything about it online doesn't make it suspect, does it? I mean she is Nigerian, so perhaps it's small and one of her relatives connected her? I must be able to find something, somewhere.' I tap the countertop with the end of my pencil, still thinking. Maybe Ashok's right. Maybe I'm too uptight. Maybe we just need to make love more often. Maybe I should worry less about getting up in time to take the boys to school. Let them be late sometimes. Let them eat Cheerios instead of French toast. Let them go to school with hair uncombed and teeth not brushed or flossed. But who am I kidding? Putting things in order is what I do best. It's who I am.

When Morayo first asked me to be the executor of her will, I joked that she would outlive me. She'd always kept herself so fit with all her walking and yoga. But sure, I said, of course I'll be your executor. So I read the will and was relieved to see that none of Morayo's money was bequeathed to me. She'd left everything to charity. That was the way it should be, I told myself. And yet a part of me still hoped that she might leave me a little gift. It wasn't that I needed it, but I longed for something to call my own, something I could deposit in our joint account and proudly say to Ashok, 'Look babe!'

I find Morayo's will in the filing cabinet and begin flipping through it as I walk back to the kitchen. There's no mention of an Abdul Rahim Centre and no mention of anything connected to Nigeria except for where it's written, 'In the event of incapacitation or death, my ex-husband, Caesar Da Silva, is to be informed.' I sit with it for some minutes, staring absently at the front page where Morayo is listed as 'resident of the City and County of San Francisco, California.' Given all the other places Morayo has lived, I wonder how she must feel when she reads that line, or the line under 'personal information' stating that she's single and doesn't have children. She's told me how much she once wanted children. I imagine that was painful.

'Don't you think you've done enough for her already?' Ashok asks, looking up from his laptop.

'Not compared to what she's done for us. Think of all the stuff she's done for the boys.'

'I know,' he sighs, 'and I'm grateful, sweetie, but she must have other friends that can help, doesn't she?'

'Not close friends that she'd trust with her bills. Not anyone else that lives here.'

'Then why doesn't she get a conservator or something?'

'A conservator, are you kidding?'

'I'm just saying.'

'Saying what? That I should abandon her? Is that what you're saying?'

'You know that's not what I'm saying.'

'Then what are you saying?'

'I'm just saying that you can't keep doing everything for her. I know you've got the biggest heart Sunny, but you just can't do everything for everybody. That's why you get so tired.'

'Well if you don't want me to be so tired then maybe you can help. Like, maybe do the laundry sometimes? Take the kids to school. Pick them up. Even just pick up your socks. That would be nice.'

Ashok closes his eyes and wearily shakes his head so that even before he says, 'Look honey, I'm sorry you think I'm a really bad husband,' I can guess what he's thinking. He's thinking, *so this is where we go from chocolate and kisses. This is what I get when I tell you to hire a cleaner; tell you to get a babysitter. Is there nothing I can suggest that makes you happy? And do you ever stop to consider what it feels like to be me? What it's like to be the sole breadwinner in this house? To be the one person everyone relies on.*

'I never said you were a terrible husband,' I snap, 'you know that's not what I was saying. I'm just saying, there's nobody else to help Morayo. Certainly nobody who would know about her stuff in Nigeria.'

11

I must have told the houseboy at least a thousand times not to disturb me with telephone calls at mealtimes. And yet here he is, hovering by the table, telling me that someone called Sunshine is on the line.

'Just take a message,' I shout. 'How many times must I remind you not to interrupt me when I'm eating? And especially not when I'm dining with my honourable good friend.'

'But, sah ...' Solomon stalls.

'What?' I snap, glancing in annoyance at the ball of eba still held between my fingers – too cold now to swallow. This wasn't the first time my houseboy was annoying me today. In the morning he'd been late with breakfast and his fruit salad had tasted of onions, suggesting that he hadn't properly washed the kitchen knives. What was going on? Had he found another job? The thought of this now disturbs me. As annoying as Solomon can sometimes be, a trustworthy houseboy is hard to come by in Lagos. So I soften my tone and tell him that unless it's the American president, this Sunshine person can wait. What kind of name is that anyway? Sunshine!

'Yes sah, I can take a message.'

'Honestly,' I sigh, shaking my head as my friend laughs at the sight of Solomon scurrying away. 'Sometimes you really have to wonder at the intelligence of these people. Now where were we?' And just as I'm dipping my eba into the sauce, Solomon returns.

'Excuse me, sah, but the person it's concerning is Mrs.'

'Then take a message. For Mrs!'

'But...'

'But what?'

'This one na for Mrs Da Silva. E no be for Madam.'

'Oh for goodness sake!' I struggle to release my napkin, wound too tightly around my neck. I keep tugging at it, brushing aside my friend's attempt to assist me. The last thing I want is for him to notice my fumbling. 'Just take the phone to the office,' I shout at Solomon, still battling to untie my napkin while trying to hide the shaking in my right hand. Once in the office, I snatch the handset from the houseboy and order the door closed behind me. What I then hear on the other end of the phone is an American accent from which I can only decipher a few words. I try inserting my hearing aid, but my wretched hand is shaking so violently and the damned thing screeching so loudly, that I have to abandon it and shout for the person to speak up. Finally, after the forever it takes the woman to inform me that Morayo is not in fact dead, my voice returns.

'Who are you, calling me from America? You can't even introduce yourself properly before you start telling me that my former wife is lying in hospital. What kind of way is that to begin a conversation? And what kind of name is "Sunshine" anyway? No, listen to me. I'm telling you, never telephone someone without introducing yourself, without explaining things properly, without putting things in context before jumping to "so-and-so had an accident". Ehn? Are you listening? What you should have said from the beginning was that she was recovering but instead you just said "accident" and "hospital", so what was I supposed to think? That someone is calling me all the way from America in the middle of the night to tell me that my wife, my ex-wife, is dead? Even now, I don't even know who you are. Who are you anyway, making me shout? Are you her nurse or what?'

'Well, Caesar, if you could just let me respond –'

'Ambassador is my title.'

'Ambassador, I was only calling to see if you might help. I was wondering if you knew of any of the Nigerian charities that Morayo supports, or might have supported over the years.'

'What?'

I sit for a moment, stunned that this woman had the audacity to drop the phone on me. How dare she! And how dare she ask me about Morayo's affairs? Was she trying to swindle me? Was this some sort of fraud? It's been years since Morayo and I were properly in touch and yet I'd just been thinking of her, as I always do around her birthday. 'Stupid me,' I find myself muttering. Why hadn't I thought to ask the woman for her number? I shouldn't have been so rude. Just this week I'd googled Morayo to see if there was anything new and then checked to see if her textbook was still in print. I remember how proud she'd been when she first published the book, one year after completing her Masters. I'd been proud of her too, but jealous of the fact that she seemed more alive in her new-found world of academia than in the embassy life that I thought we shared. The fact that I hadn't encouraged her was my mistake. Except that I didn't realize my mistake until it was too late. One day, out of nowhere, she announced that she was leaving. I got home from work and there she was, suitcase already packed. 'Go then!' I'd shouted more out of consternation than anger. For years I'd blamed her for our separation; whenever people asked why she'd left, I told them she'd had a nervous breakdown just like her mother, brought on by the death of her father. It was easier to blame her than having to examine the ways in which I'd failed her, and especially so when rumours of past affairs began to surface. Some people were even suggesting that the reason Morayo had gone to live in San Francisco was because she'd fallen in love with a woman. If this were so, then there was nothing I could have done to save our marriage. If she was born attracted to women then what difference did it make that

I'd been married before, or that I wasn't able to give her children, or that my job had ceased to be of interest to her. It meant that her initial attraction to me must have been based on something other than love. Perhaps she saw me simply as a means to an end – as a way of living outside of Nigeria and travelling the world. But deep down I always knew that I couldn't escape blame that easily. Whether or not any of the rumours were true, I knew that there was a time when our love for each other was real. I remember the funny way she had of laughing through her nose. The eyebrows. Mischievous. Sensuous. I remember the warmth in her hands and the cold in her feet. Those feet that used to chase mine under the sheets. More than fifteen years we'd been together, M. and I. And after we parted she never did remarry. I thought she would, but she didn't. Feeling discomfort beneath my eyelids I squeeze my eyes shut and instinctively pat my shirt pocket looking for eye drops. I tilt my head back ready to moisten, only to be surprised. My eyes were already watering.

12

'Bless you darling, bless you,' I keep saying, because Sunshine is here and has brought me books. 'Bless you!' Then seeing that she hasn't sat down, I offer her the choice between commode and grubby looking armchair. Knowing how fussy my friend can be, I smile as she chooses instead to perch on the edge of the bed next to me. She'll be worried about touching anything too dirty but she may also be afraid of hurting my hip so I demonstrate how strong I am by shifting from left to right, proving that she needn't be so tentative around my body. Then I tell her that had she come earlier she would have met the man responsible for my speedy recovery. I describe my last session with the physical therapist, getting her to picture the lengths to which he goes in order to be discreet while holding my hips in alignment. I recount how politely he instructs me to 'clench my glutes', while I'm busy worrying over how I might prevent myself from inadvertently passing gas when undertaking such physical exertions. I may be old, but farting and burping in public is not something I intend to succumb to. If I can help it. Sunshine laughs and I joke that the poor man need not worry about an old woman like me. It's not as if I'm going to mistake his touch for one of flirtation, or even want to flirt with him in the first place. But the latter isn't true. I *am* flirting when I joke about my creaky knees and stiff joints, all the while hoping he'll compliment me on what good shape I'm in. And whether or not he's aware that I'd like him to congratulate me on my fitness (but who am I kidding, of course he knows), I thrive on his praise, diligently doing all my assigned exercises and more.

'Had I met the man twenty years ago,' I tell Sunshine, 'he would've been smitten. One glance at my tight glutes and my curvy hips, and he wouldn't have been able to resist. He would've had my name tattooed right across his chest.'

'And you? Where would you have tattooed his?' Sunshine smiles.

'Oh, well, if anywhere, under my thumbs. Symbolically,' I chuckle. 'But speaking of tattoos, he's actually offered to introduce me to his tattoo artist.'

'*You* want a tattoo?'

'I do.'

Sunshine looks shocked. 'You mean that while I've been trying to convince Zach that tattoos aren't cool, you, his honorary grandmother, are about to get one?'

'But you're assuming I don't have one already?'

'Do you?'

'No,' I laugh. 'But you know, when I was young, everyone had tattoos. And by that I mean the facial markings that told you where someone came from. So not exactly tattoos in the modern sense, although we did have some of those too. Sometimes women had these green tattoos written on the inside of their arms. They were all just forms of bodily adornment. But by the time I was born, people started thinking that both the facial markings and the love tattoos, as I like to call them, were primitive. I wanted a tattoo, but wasn't allowed one. And now tattoos are everywhere, everyone's writing on the body.'

'And you still want one? On your face?'

'Oh no, not on my face, darling. Too many wrinkles there and besides, you need some elasticity for a good tattoo. But there are many other sweet spots on this body of mine.'

'Like?'

'Like you'll have to wait and see,' I smile. 'Now, tell me, how are you, and my tattoo-free boys?'

I worry about Sunshine sometimes, in her family of men and boys. I like Ashok but I fear that Sunshine is too easily swayed by what he thinks and too eager to please him. I see some of my younger self in Sunshine and try to encourage her to have more of her own mind. But I also try not to be too overbearing.

When Morayo asks me how I am, I tell her that I'm fine. 'Although Ashok is still trying to persuade me to go back to school.' I pause, hoping that Morayo will reassure me by saying that Ashok is wrong and that I shouldn't feel pressured into going to grad school. But she doesn't comment so I reluctantly return to talking about the boys. I tell her how Avi is coming along with his New Year's 'revolutions', which makes her laugh. Then I talk about Zach, how he's started rowing which means that three early mornings a week I drive him to Marin and back. I pull out my phone to share some recent photographs. Morayo, who must have also noticed me checking the time, tells me that I mustn't feel obliged to stay. Feeling guilty, I insist that I'm not in a rush.

'I know, darling,' she says. 'I'm just looking for an excuse to start reading all these lovely books you've brought for me.' She winks then peers into the bag. 'Auster and Angelou, that's lovely, and these?' she asks, looking quizzically at the others. 'What are these? They look like Mills & Boon.' She points to the boxed set.

'You tell me,' I smile, 'I found them by your bed.' I think that Morayo is only feigning surprise, but no, it seems that she really doesn't recognize them.

'Ahh,' she says, after some moments. 'These must have come from the house cleaner. Did you ever meet Tina? Bless her. She knew I liked books so she was always bringing me more, only not the sort that I liked to read. And then, of course, I could never get rid of them because she would've noticed. But now that you've brought them, perhaps I should read them. What do you reckon?'

'You have a house cleaner?'

'Oh, I used to, darling, long time ago. And I know. I know my place is a bit of a mess right now, but being here has given me time to think. It's funny, you know, as you get older, you begin to see yourself becoming more like your parents. After my father retired I remember him staying at home, not wanting to do much but listen to his radio. He didn't want to get rid of anything and so the house just got more and more cluttered. So you're right, my house could probably use a good sort out and even a cleaner again, but I'll get to it, I promise.'

'Well, as a matter of fact, I've done some of that for you already.'

'Oh Sunshine! You shouldn't have!'

'No, that's okay. It's just that there were a lot of things in the apartment that needed attention. Like there was a letter from the DMV, do you remember? A bunch of bills and also some bank transactions. Ashok and I got a little bit worried by one of them.'

'Yes,' Morayo interrupts. 'I know what you must have seen. The payments to a certain charity which turned out to be an scam?'

I nod, feeling relieved that at least she's aware of it.

'It was a silly mistake Sunshine, and although I'm embarrassed, I'm glad you now know. I'm actually relieved that you know. I should've been more careful, but I'm dealing with it now, darling. I've talked to the bank and it won't happen again.'

'Well there's certainly no need to be embarrassed; God knows how many embarrassing things I've shared with you over the years. But you should have told us, we could have helped. Ashok deals with that sort of thing all the time.'

'I know, Sunshine. It's just that I'm usually so careful, but that particular email just got me. It didn't have any of the usual hallmarks of scam mail – no funny spelling errors or formal salutations, so it never crossed my mind that this might be another prank. And you know how upset I've been by everything happening in Nigeria recently. So when that email came, I just believed it was genuine. I thought the money would go to the victims. But then, of course, when I realized my mistake, well I didn't want to bother you. You have enough on your plate as it is. I'll be much more vigilant from now on, I promise.'

'But I'm always here for you, Morayo, and so is Ashok.'

'I know, darling, and I'm grateful, I am.'

'So look,' I say, seizing my chance. 'You know how you just mentioned that your apartment needs cleaning? Which means it's not just me being OCD, right? So while you were in hospital I got a friend to help me sort through some of your stuff, the stuff you don't need.'

'Stuff?'

'Well mostly, like old papers. Except unfortunately, there was a small misunderstanding and some of your books, but just a few, got thrown out.'

'My books!' Morayo exclaims.

'Just some. And only those that were falling apart. You had mice in your apartment, Morayo, and they were eating your papers and even some of your books.' I hesitate, but seeing her alarm I keep talking. 'I asked Francisco to get rid of the old papers because they were in a really bad state. Remember how we'd sorted through them last year? But then, unfortunately –'

'You got rid of things without me being there!' she cries, her face darkening with disbelief.

'I didn't want to, Morayo, but it was unhygienic and I just thought it would be helpful.'

'Helpful?' she shouts. 'But why couldn't you wait? How could you possibly know what's important to me and what's not? That's my life, Sunshine! My books!'

'I'm sorry, Morayo, I'm sorry. I was trying to help. You've just got so many books. You've even got more than one copy of some of them.'

'Well of course I do! Just like you have dozens of pairs of yoga pants and lipsticks and shoes, don't you? How would you feel if someone went through all your "stuff" and got rid of what they thought were just duplicates or extras? Just because *you* would never buy more than one fucking book doesn't mean others wouldn't. Doesn't mean there isn't a very good reason why I do!'

'That's not what I meant,' I stammer, thrown by her swearing. 'I said I'm sorry. And when it happened I did my best to get it all back. I don't know what else to say.'

'But what's "sorry" going to do? How's that supposed to help? It was just reckless of you. Stupid and thoughtless.'

'Thoughtless?' I cry, snatching my bag and car keys. 'Yes, okay, I'm stupid and thoughtless and you'd probably be much better off with a conservator.'

13

At first, all I could do was to stare at the door after it banged shut. Then I let out such a cry of anguish that Bella must have heard me from outside.

'What happened?' Bella calls, panic in her voice as she runs in. She tugs at the sheet covering my head. 'Did you fall?'

'No,' I manage, turning reluctantly from where I'd buried my face in the pillow. 'I'm okay.'

'Your friend has gone?'

Yes, I nod, trying not to start crying again. Bella takes my hand. 'I'm sorry,' she says. 'You know, sometimes it's good to cry. Let it all come out.'

And for several more minutes this is all that passes between us, me sobbing and she squeezing my hand.

And then Bella tells me that God loves me, which almost sets me off again.

'I think it makes a difference to believe in God,' she says, 'because the people who don't trust God, when those people are getting old it's more difficult because they get angry. Everything is bothering them and they don't understand the rest of the people.'

I nod, reminded of my father, as she speaks.

'I think,' she says, 'well, I was thinking of building a place in my country. You know, a place for getting old. But better than here, because in my country, in Nicaragua, you have already sunshine and good food, you have already good music and beautiful flowers and books, you know.' She stands up now to tidy the books she has seen caught beneath my bedcovers. 'So you must come to visit me in my country.'

'I'd love to, Bella,' I say, and making an effort to appear cheerful, I cautiously swing both legs out of bed.

'And tonight you'll go to dinner, no?' Bella pats my hand.

'I'll try.' I manage a smile. No more moping around, I tell myself. No more doubting. I mustn't let this get me down. I must simply get myself home and have a proper sort out with the DMV, the bank, and my apartment. As we hug I'm enveloped by her sweet perfume.

'Dulce y Cabana,' she tells me when I ask, and I know from her smile that she knows that I know what this is. She knows that I recognize it as expensive, as having class.

She's told me that her life has not always been as hard as it is now. That once upon a time she used to live in New York, in midtown Manhattan, where she was able to afford many things, even her own maid. She's also told me that she holds a university degree, as do her brothers and sisters, many of whom own mansions in Managua.

'Dulce y Cabana,' I repeat, deliberately echoing Bella's mispronunciation. 'Sweet shelter, how perfect.' And then the phone rings. 'It's my friend,' I whisper, covering the handset. 'It's Sunshine.'

'Sunshine is good!' she whispers back, as she waves goodbye.

I apologize to Sunshine for having shouted at her. I admit that I overreacted and that, contrary to how it might have appeared, I appreciate what she was trying to do for me. 'Books can always be replaced,' I say, hoping she'll sense how difficult this is for me to acknowledge, let alone believe. But she doesn't seem to notice. And now I'm fed up of listening to her sobbing down the phone, yet I'm still trying to be the mature and wise one because that is what I'm supposed to be at this age. I remind myself that Sunshine is still young and has her hands full with looking after the children. I'm older and ought to be wiser. I should understand that she was just careless and not deliberately trying to hurt me, not even when she suggested a conservator. But I'd told her so many fucking times, that I never wanted to be looked after by strangers. I'd told her more than once that if it ever came to that I would prefer to find a way of quietly slipping into that good night ahead of time. She knows this. And while I understand that what she said earlier was uttered in a moment of anger, I now have no faith that when the time comes she will honour my wishes. But I'm tired of crying, so after we say our goodbyes I make my way to the sink and wash my face. No point in wallowing in self-pity. What is done is done and I'll wait until I get home to see how bad things really are. Consider the birds in the sky, I remind myself. Consider the birds in the sky.

To cheer myself up I decide to dress nicely for dinner. Thinking of my red leather jacket, I look for it in the wardrobe. 'Red-leather-yellow-leather,' I whisper, reminded of a childhood game. But whoever did my packing had only packed dull-looking clothing. The only colourful items are a green T-shirt and a Walt Disney sweater, neither of which belong to me. It makes me wonder if some of my own clothes might be hanging in other people's wardrobes. I also wonder if this strange looking T-shirt and sweater might belong to people recently deceased. 'All the more reason then, to dress with panache while I still can,' I announce, while choosing trousers and a loose fitting blouse, neither of which flatter my figure. But once I've twisted my hair into bantu knots and added the lipstick, I don't look too bad. Antonio always liked my red lipstick. Chanel was his choice. So now I'm ready. Except. One more thing. A book. This way, if I'm unlucky enough to sit next to someone crazy, then at least I'll have something to read.

When I arrive in the dining hall, someone's phone is ringing and because it's a catchy ringtone, I take a few jaunty steps and sing along.

'Ain't nothin' but a hound dog.
Cryin' all the time.'

When I was younger, I used to be sceptical of old people who claimed to feel 'as good as new' but here I am thinking exactly that. My hips are getting better and Elvis has put me in the mood for a bottle of Chablis. Now, instead of wearing nondescript trousers with a cotton blouse, I imagine I'm dressed in one of my cocktail dresses – the yellow chiffon with dotted Swiss, for example. Or better still, I've glided in on my white peau de soie gown, the one with gold trim at the waist and an open back. This would explain why everyone has now turned to stare. For it was Antonio's favourite too; though it might not have been, had I confessed that the dress was an anniversary gift from Caesar. The Home's steamy dining hall disappears, replaced by the foyer of our house in Chanakyapuri.

This was my favourite of all the ambassadorial residences with its modern design and tropical gardens that always reminded me of Lagos. I'm standing by the entrance, which is tastefully decorated with paintings and sculptures. Caesar believed in showcasing the best of Nigerian art and because he had such a good eye we were owners of works by Enwonwu and Onobrakpeya even before they became well known. This is the house where, in the early 1970s, we hosted our first head of state dinner with senior Indian ministers, business leaders, and other ambassadors. So here I am, greeting guests with a touch of my gloved hand or the offer of a cheek for those who preferred to go with kisses. 'Good evening sir! Welcome. Welcome madame, what a delight to see you again. Ambassador, what an honour – please do come and meet our head of state.' And all the while

I'm busy casting an expert eye over the floral arrangements of orchids and bird of paradise and watching my staff weave gracefully amongst our guests balancing spicy canapés on silver trays. I make mental notes of various people I wish to introduce to others, as well as where I might reseat the lone bachelor who was invited for the sole purpose of equalling out the number of men to women around the dinner table. Rather than place him next to the banker's wife as I'd been instructed, I now decide to seat him next to pretty Olivia, who looks thoroughly fed up with her ever-pontificating ambassador husband. And so the evening continues, as such functions did, filled with superficial chit-chat until the men retired to discuss the *important* things and the women were left gossiping and complaining about their servants. Then I would sneak off for a smoke in the gardens or a protracted visit to the powder room where I always kept a book of poetry. It was rare that I found myself missing the pomp and ceremony of those evenings, and yet tonight I long for just a moment of that time when I might enter a room and know that heads would turn. Know that every member of my staff would be attentive to even my smallest, most discreet request. Know that as hostess I had some power, at the very least, to request a drink. So what's the worst that will happen if I now ask for a glass of wine? Still dancing, I make my way to an empty table, not noticing at first that people have started running. In the commotion that follows, I feel someone grab hold of my wrist. I think it's an earthquake so I try ducking beneath a table. Then I feel someone lift me up.

'My walker?' I ask. 'You mean all of this fuss is just because I left my walker behind?'

14

I was already sitting down with Pearl when I saw what happened to Morayo – saw the staff rushing towards her, the shock on her face and her embarrassment at being placed in a wheelchair. Now they've brought her to our table and I don't know what to say. Whether to try reassuring her or just pretend not to have noticed to save her any further embarrassment. 'Don't mind the staff,' I find myself saying. 'They're always afraid of getting sued. That's all it is. I've seen you walking perfectly fine in the hallways. All that panic back there. Completely needless. And please excuse Pearl's clapping, she gets a little excited whenever there's a bit of commotion.'

After we've been given our plates (tonight it's curry) I pass the basketful of poppadums to Morayo. I'm pleased to see that she's enjoying the food and I tell her that the menus are always much better with the substitute chef. The regular cook is away on vacation. When she asks me how I know these things, I explain that I've been coming here for almost a year. 'I'm here to be with Pearl who has Parkinson's disease with memory loss. She's doing much better now. Now that she's in the care of others more skilled than me.' I turn to Pearl but as she's not paying attention I return to Morayo. 'The worst part for Pearl, well for both of us, was when she knew that she was forgetting things. That was very hard, but now we're past that stage, so it's much less stressful.' I add, making an effort to sound cheerful while aware that Pearl has now started blowing kisses to the man across the room.

'It must be hard,' Morayo says, 'but I can see that you have a very calming effect on her.'

'That's kind of you,' I smile, knowing that sometimes Pearl goes further, trying to actually kiss these men. It's not Pearl's fault and she's not deliberately trying to hurt me, but I still feel betrayed when she does it. 'You seem to be the calm one,' I say to Morayo, hoping to distract her from observing Pearl's antics. 'You didn't seem flustered earlier. Right through all the alarm, you stayed serene.'

'The verb 'dazed' might be the better word to describe it, I think,' she replies. 'I actually thought we were having an earthquake. But I do like that word serene. It's almost as if you could fly or float on it. Ser-eeeene.'

I watch, bemused, as she stretches out her arms mimicking flight. 'May I ask, what you're reading?'

'It's called *Winter Journal*,' she sighs, pulling out the book from where it was tucked into the side of her wheelchair.

And because I'm not sure whether she's sighing because of what happened earlier or because she'd rather not talk about the book, I mutter again about how annoying the staff can sometimes be.

'It's just been one of those days,' she says, insisting that I take the book. 'It's one of Paul Auster's. Do you know him?'

I shake my head. 'I'm afraid I don't read much fiction, but Pearl used to and still does, in her own way. It's a shame she's not in a state to talk to you about it now. I'm sure she would have heard of this author.' I say, even though I suspect she wouldn't have. Pearl liked mysteries and romance novels, and this doesn't look like one of those sorts of books. But I don't see anything wrong with making Pearl seem more literary now that her dementia has reduced her to such an infantile state. And as if agreeing with me, Pearl returns to us and leans over to peer at the book. We look together and I glimpse some handwritten notes at the back. 'Are these yours?' I ask, before realizing that my question might be perceived as nosy.

'They're nothing really, just my own attempts at copying the author's style,' Morayo explains before retrieving the book.

'Come,' I call to Pearl who doesn't want to let go of the book and now stands next to it with Morayo.

'Would you like me to read to you?' Morayo asks Pearl.

Pearl smiles and Morayo hesitates, looking to me for confirmation. But when Pearl sits down next to her and looks up, expectantly, there's no question of what Pearl wants. I'm embarrassed both by Pearl's juvenile behaviour and by the fact that I'm embarrassed, but Morayo doesn't seem to notice. She smiles at Pearl and invites her to choose a page. Then she reads a passage and explains to both of us that there's something in the author's way of describing his life through the history of his body that she admires. 'It's what inspired me,' she says, 'to do the same, but from a woman's perspective.' And then addressing Pearl she asks if she'd like to hear more. This time she reads from her own notes. 'Your body,' she begins, 'happily crouched next to bushes and shrubs, pruning, trimming, and always checking for beetles and whitefly. Your body bending to turn the mattress, to make the bed, put clothes in the washing machine then hoisting the heavy hamper onto your hip. Your body bending and stretching to hang each item upside down on the clothesline with the pegs carried in your mouth. Your body as a girl, tumbling and rolling and headstanding and cartwheeling and tottering around in mummy's canoe-sized shoes. Your body,' but here she stops as Pearl begins to clap.

'You write beautifully,' I tell Morayo. 'And Pearl, I think, is under the impression that she's the author.'

'Well that's wonderful,' she smiles, as Pearl takes a bow and resumes the blowing of kisses. 'It makes me realize just how much I miss my students. But is she okay?' Morayo asks, looking concerned now that Pearl is wandering off.

'She'll be fine,' I explain. 'Tonight is music night and Pearl loves to sing. And the staff are watching her, do you see? It's the one thing that she doesn't forget. But back to books, would you be able to give me some tips? I have lots of spare time these days so it would be good to do some reading.'

'Well,' she smiles, 'I used to be an English professor so my lists tend to be long and also not very contemporary.'

'Perfect,' I say, 'I'm not exactly contemporary myself.' Such conversations, I realize, are what I've been missing. How refreshing it is to talk of things that have nothing to do with aches and pains or the status of an illness. Cancer. Diabetes. Dementia. And she speaks with such authority on literature. But it's not just the content of what she says that I'm enjoying: it's also the gentle lilt of her voice and the thoughtfulness with which she ponders what she says. The way her hands move in sync with her words. She has nicely manicured nails, which speak to her elegance and sophistication. She begins with well-known works, some of which I'd once read at school but have since forgotten. And then she lists her favourite African authors followed by some from the Caribbean. She asks if that's where I'm from.

'Yes, good guess,' I smile, 'I come from Guyana, but I'm afraid that I know very little about our writers and not even about the more famous ones in the region like Walcott and Rhys.' I hope that my name-dropping comes across well. 'So it's about time I read them and I'm sure I can find some in the library.'

'Or I can always lend them to you,' she offers, pausing for a moment before asking what it is that I do.

'What does Reggie do?' I repeat. 'Well, like you, I'm also an academic. Or was, before I retired. I taught courses on political and economic development with a focus on the Caribbean. But unlike you, I can't honestly say I miss teaching. I do miss the academic environment though.' And then I change the subject, afraid that she might ask more. I don't want to have to admit that I was never given tenure. As Morayo seems particularly interested in where I come from, I tell her about my childhood and then how Pearl and I first met. I'm flattered by her interest, and especially so given that nobody else has asked about my life in all the time that I've been coming to the Home. I'm wise enough though not to let the conversation linger for too long on me. I remember my mother saying, 'Don't be fooled, Reginald, into thinking that woman is lovin' the sound of your voice, man. Most women is jus' waitin' for the man to shut up.' So I ask her how long she's been a professor and what she did before that. I marvel at the many places where she's lived. She tells me she was once a diplomat's wife. I tell her that this doesn't surprise me given her grace, but she insists that she wasn't the most graceful of diplomat wives.

'Well, for one thing, I could never get terribly excited about menu planning and all the protocol one had to observe,' she says, 'so that didn't really make for a good hostess. And those sorts of things were important back then. But more than that, I think I'm just not a natural diplomat.'

'Is that a bad thing?'

'For an ambassador's wife it is,' she sighs, 'whereas for teaching I suppose I found it useful. I do miss my students. Do you have children, Reggie?'

'I have a son, Anthony. He got his MBA and now works at Goldman Sachs; much brighter than his old man. And Pearl has four. And you?'

'No, no children of my own, although at times many of my students felt like my children. And I do like the name Anthony.'

15

I thought, of course, of Antonio when Reggie mentioned me his son's name, and I was imagining how nice it would be to travel back to that part of the world when I noticed that the dining room had emptied. We were now the last ones there. 'We should be leaving,' I say, thinking that Reggie would need to say goodbye to his wife and that I should be getting back to my room. 'Oh, I think I can walk now, don't you? Besides nobody's around.' I remark, having forgotten all about the wretched wheelchair until he gallantly steps behind me, ready to push.

'But the staff might just suddenly appear if you start walking on your own,' he says. 'I would offer you a piggyback, but you're taller than me.'

'And heavier too!' I laugh. 'Which means you might drop me and then that would really give the staff cause for alarm. Not that I'm doubting your strength, of course.'

'No, of course not,' he laughs. 'You're far too diplomatic for that.'

'Well exactly! Gosh, I can't even remember the last time I had a piggyback.' But then I do.

It was in London, 1 October 1965. Nigeria's Independence Day. I was at a glamorous party, sprinkled with the cream of the Lagos jet set, at the centre of which stood Caesar – the reason I was there. We'd met a few weeks earlier at the British Council where Caesar was the invited speaker. Caesar meticulously turned out in a crisp white shirt and tantalizing aftershave – ever attentive, always the diplomat, living up to his imperial namesake. He was so tall and lean and with such high cheekbones, all of which added to his air of effortless sophistication. It seemed almost too good to be true that I, amongst the many, was the one he'd chosen. And after the party, he invited me to his hotel. It was raining so he'd lifted me onto his back, saving my dainty, black suede shoes from getting wet; shoes that I'd bought specially for that night. And while we waited for a taxi, I looped my arms around his neck and breathed him in – every ounce of him: his Brylcreem, aftershave and cigarettes. He leant back to nestle my cheek and bounced me gently on his back. Later, at the Dorchester, we would bounce together on top of white sheets while I anxiously held my breath. It was my first time, and I was embarrassed by the noise the bed was making, afraid that others might hear. Nobody had warned me that I would bleed, so this is what I remember: Caesar covering the bloodstained sheets with a towel and then wrapping me warmly in the blankets. He had withdrawn early so no need to worry, he'd said lovingly. But of course I was terrified, and everyday thereafter I found myself checking for the blood of my menstrual cycle and praying for my bleeding to resume; if I were to fall pregnant what shame this would bring to my father. Caesar joked that he was probably too old, in any case, to have children. He was my rock in those days, so I never suspected that the reason he didn't mind not having children was because he already had children of his own.

I'd been married to Caesar for several years before he told me that my way of making love was 'motherly'. Motherly. Of all the words he could have chosen. It hit me in the gut, right there in the uterus. 'I don't mean that as a criticism,' he'd added. 'It's just what I've noticed.' For having slept with more than one he could make such observations, whereas I, having only slept with him, well what would I know? But I could feel that something was wrong in the way he kissed me: the way his tongue thrust ever deeper, impatient with my reticence, as it flicked and plunged, unsatisfied back and forth. I sensed from him a yearning for love more urgent and erotic, and felt wretched for not being able to reciprocate. One morning, unable to continue with the pretence of enjoying our twice weekly copulation, I bit his lip hard so that it bled and instead of stopping to daub it clean, to kiss it gently better in a motherly way, I ignored the cut and thrust my tongue deep into his mouth. I wanted him to back off. I wanted him to be more tender and patient, but instead he mistook my anger as passion and rose to an occasion of only his own imagination. How could I explain that the way he craved my body made me angry?

In contrast, Antonio's tenderness and the timid uncertainty with which he occasionally dared to touch me made me feel alive. Often, when the world sat enthralled, leaning in to catch Caesar's words, I would lean out, imagining some far away place, in a distant galaxy where no one else existed but Antonio. It was only occasionally that Antonio and I would meet and stray out of sight of others, and although we always kept things within the confines of kissing and fondling, stopping short of undressing, this prolonged restraint made us all the more desperate for each other. We both knew that one day we would go further, that in some highly erotic or romantic moment we would jettison all the reasons that got in our way and just get on with it. We might find ourselves rolling in an English meadow or on some breath-taking Mediterranean beach or, for nostalgia's sake, in the back of a cinema a few empty rows behind everyone else. Or, what the hell, we would sit wherever we pleased. Let anyone who found us too distracting move to other seats. Or let them stay if they wished and watch us: bodies entangled and moving as two, then one, while the film danced off our backs. But in the end, of course, the location for our first lovemaking was neither glamorous nor risqué, but in Antonio's nondescript Parisian hotel beneath instructions of where to run in the event of a fire. There, in room 212, behind the hastily hung 'Do Not Disturb' sign, I undid my gown and let it drop to the floor before reaching to steady Antonio. Holding him gently, I stroked the lapels of his pale blue shirt before ripping it open, surprising a dozen white buttons that popped like champagne, as the two of us stumbled, hungrily to the carpeted floor.

As we wait for the elevator that will take us back to our rooms, Reggie, with his hands resting on the back of the wheelchair, asks what I plan to do for my birthday.

'Intuition,' he smiles, when I ask him how he knows. Then he points to the noticeboard next to the elevator that's too far away for me to read, but where he tells me that all the birthdays for the month are listed. 'The kitchen will buy you a cake. So all you need to do is tell them what you'd like. You can even request the number of candles.'

'Well, sitting in this wheelchair makes me feel like a hundred and one,' I laugh. 'So let's just hope they have enough candles.'

I'd almost forgotten about my birthday. How depressing to think that I might have to spend it here. Surely, I wouldn't still be here next week? The PT had said I should be home in a few days, so I cling to that. But, nevertheless, just in case, shortly after Reggie drops me off, I head back down to the dining hall. No wheelchair this time and no bloody walker either.

16

Being a chef at an old folks' home isn't glamorous. It's not like cooking at some fancy restaurant with celebrities coming in and hooking you up. It's nothing like that. No famous people here, unless you count the mother of some opera singer, but I ain't never seen her. Only opera person I know is Pavarotti, and he's dead, right? Basically there's nothing glamorous here on the clientele front and the food isn't fancy either. No caviar, no foie gras, no truffles, although, now that I'm thinking about it that would be kinda ideal for old folks – soft to chew, easy on the stomach. But I have to make do with just the basics and that's cool with me. I didn't learn at the Cordon Bleu. I learned from my mama then got a credential from the Man. But my real cred, my street cred, is from my building and my mom. Turning ordinary food into crack food is what I do. Just one hit of my cooking and you gotta come back for more. Besides, the expectations are so low here; it's not hard to beat. Plus there's no real pressure – everyone gets served the same thing at the same time. All I got to do is stay within budget and make sure meals are nutritionally balanced and don't make nobody sick. Old people with the runs ain't good. The director lets me know that when I'm doing the cooking he never gets complaints – no notes dropped in the complaint box. But I don't need him to tell me that. I can see how much they like my food here by how little comes back. I'm the celebrity chef around here. 'Shit!' I say, startled to find a woman, out of nowhere, suddenly standing beside me. How long had she been there while I was busy talking shit to myself? 'S'cuse my French, ma'am, but I didn't know you was there. You okay? You lost or something?'

'I'm sorry for scaring you,' she says, while looking at me like maybe I'm the crazy one.

'Naw, you didn't scare me. I just wasn't expecting it, that's all.'

'I came to thank you for tonight's dinner. It was delicious.'

'Thanks,' I smile. 'That's the first time someone's done that. I appreciate it.'

'So what's your secret? Because from what I hear, you're the best cook in town.'

'Cuz of what you heard me saying back then?'

'No, from what everyone here says.'

'Really? Well I just like making people happy how I know best and that's with food. Anyway, I'm Toussaint.'

'Pleased to meet you, Toussaint,' she says, giving my hand a firm shake. 'I'm Morayo. And I like your name, Toussaint.'

'Well that's my mom. She was a history teacher so that's how she chose my name. But you're not from here, right?'

'No. I'm just recuperating.'

'It's just that your accent sounded different.'

'Oh,' she laughs, 'I thought you were asking me whether I live here, in the Home. But Nigeria, that's where I come from. Originally.'

'For real? Africa, word! That's cool. My mom always wanted to take us to the motherland. So what's it like?' I ask, while I reach to turn the radio off. Then I change my mind and search for a different station. 'Cuz I've always wanted to know about Africa. You know, I hear all these things but I don't know what it's really like.'

'It's like everywhere, Toussaint. It's amazing, crazy, wonderful, and frustrating – sometimes all at the same time.'

'And racist like here?'

'No, it's not. Other parts of the continent are but not West Africa. You must come and visit one day, Toussaint.'

And there, she does it again, pronouncing my name so nice before she tells me more about Africa. 'For sure, I'd love to go,' I tell her, smiling as I look at her feet tapping to the music. 'And y'all have good music in Africa, right? Isn't that where Fela comes from?'

'Ain't no doubt about it,' she says, singing along to the song now playing on the radio.

'You know this song?' I ask, raising the volume while watching how she's swinging her hips and clicking her fingers.

'Evelyn Champagne King!'

She's kicked off her shoes and I see some toe rings and I wonder just how old she is. Her right sleeve has slipped a little from her shoulder as she grooves to the right, showing a slim hot pink bra strap. I raise my eyebrows surprised that someone her age would wear such a thing. I'm getting a little worked up as I watch her move, which surprises me and scares me. 'So what's the food like in Africa?'

'Well, I'm not a cook, but I do love to eat and there's such an incredible variety of foods in the continent. As for Nigeria, there's so much delicious food, it's hard to know where to start. But a lot of the food is spicy which is why I really loved what you made tonight. Where do you get your inspiration?'

'Oh man, I'd love to travel more and get even more inspiration, but for now I guess I just learn what I can from the way my mom used to cook and then from tasting different things in different places. I like to experiment and kinda make my own dishes. I guess I think a lot about what will taste good and work all of our senses. You know, the way the food smells, and the way I present it on the plate. And cooking in a place like here I try to take into account the restrictions that I know about, from having lived with my grandmother. So like if people wear dentures then that means the food can't be too chewy. Poor digestion means the food shouldn't be too spicy and you need to go easy on the onions. So that's why, to be honest with you, if I'd been cooking tonight's curry just for me, it would've been a lot hotter. But just to make sure it's okay with everyone I kinda toned it down, but still kept it tasty.'

'So do you get to choose what you cook or do you follow a set menu?'

'Well, usually the regular chef writes the menu for the week but seeing that he's gone I can kinda improvise a little bit, as long as we have the ingredients. To be honest with you I don't really like the suggested menu. It's boring and old-fashioned. Most of the time I try to change it. So like today ...' I pause to fetch the menu so that I can show her what I mean. 'So like, today we're supposed to be having a herb green salad and herbed grilled chicken with a four onion quiche and apple pie. But right there, I mean, you can't have two herby things and then two tarts! There's no variety in that. Besides, nobody should be having four onion anything, anywhere in my opinion. So I changed it up. It's like my culinary mix tape; the tracks may be familiar but the beats, fades, and mixes are all mine. Made a light curry and fresh fruit salad. And then I also like to think about the weather and create food that matches that too. So like for the birthday dinner next week, you can see that the guy has catch of the day with buttered noodles, but that sounds too heavy. And fish in my opinion just doesn't go with noodles, so if I'm still covering next week I might do something like smoked fish tacos and then make something more of the dessert. But not a peach melba, like it's suggested. I mean just cuz folks are old here, not you I mean, but others, it doesn't mean the food has to be old-fashioned, right? So maybe I'll do a black forest gateau or some kind of tart maybe.'

'Well if I'm still here next week then I really hope you'll be here too because it's my birthday.'

'For real? Okay, so I'm gonna make something really *extra* special. What would you like? Like a carrot cake or a chocolate cake? I could even do doughnuts or cupcakes if you like those better.'

'You know what I'd really like, Toussaint?'

'Tell me,' I say, now thinking I'll surprise her with something from her country, like some African fruit from the Muslim market or the Asia food store.

'So what I'd really like would be for my friend, Amirah, to make some baklava. I'd just need someone to pick it up for me. But that's what I'd love. It is such divine baklava. You'd love it, Toussaint.'

'Sure,' I tell her. 'I'm sure we can do that.'

'Fabulous,' she winks.

'Fabulous,' I repeat, and before I can check myself, I'm winking back.

17

When he asked me what Africa was like I told him all the wonderful things, reminding him, as I always reminded my students, that Africa wasn't a country but a continent as varied, if not more so, as Europe. I wanted him to feel proud of where his ancestors came from. I wanted him to know that there are places in the world where a black man doesn't have to walk around fearing the colour of his skin. So I told Toussaint all the good things – the weather, the food, the spectacular landscapes, but above all I spoke of the warmth of Africa's people. Told him how modern the continent is, how he could go to malls just like he does in America. 'So one day,' I said, 'when you decide to visit, just let me know and I'll hook you up.' Hook you up, I'd offered, as though I were his age, speaking in his lingo – even though these days I know nobody his age to put him in touch with. I was inviting him not just to Nigeria, but also to the whole continent, as if the continent were my personal possession, my home. I was inviting him as though he were family, as though he were my son.

Now, as I lie in bed, I close my eyes to better picture my shelves with the spines of my literary friends. I am making a mental list of the books I will lend to Toussaint. I think of James Baldwin, Ralph Ellison, and Earnest Gaines as well as C.L.R. James. I suspect, however, that Toussaint's mother will have already made him read the *The Black Jacobins,* so that one might not be necessary. And with his interest in Africa I could maybe give him some books on Nigeria. I have a few on Fela. And what about books relating to cooking and chefs? I could lend him *The Famished Road* and another book by Zola whose title escapes me. Memory. All of this was assuming that Toussaint had a real passion for food. But what if he didn't? What if he didn't really enjoy his job? What if he was only working to make ends meet? What if he'd like a different career, a better career? I fall asleep still thinking of him and my books.

The next morning, smiling at the swiftly vanishing threads of my dream, I go to search for Toussaint. He's not in the kitchen so I return to the dining hall and sit with Pearl and Reggie.

'Where's our wonderful chef?' Pearl asks, mimicking what I've just asked Reggie.

'He's not here yet, darling,' Reggie answers.

'Where'd he go?' Pearl persists.

'I don't know, honey.'

'Honey?' asks another woman at the table.

'Honey honey, touch me baby, ah-hah,' Pearl sings.

'Honey?' the other woman repeats, looking for it.

'No, Donna, nobody's asking for the honey,' Reggie explains. 'Have you got your HEARING AID in? Donna?'

'Honey honey, hold me baby, ah-hah.'

Madness, I think to myself. It's madness here, madness. Madness. Old age is a massacre. No place for sissies. No place for love songs. No place for dreaming. No place for dreaming erotic dreams about a man half my age. And because I'm distracted, I'm slow to notice what's going on around me until an angry voice draws me back.

'What do you see when you see black folks?' the man shouts. 'They're either in prison or they're walking around, pants hanging down their butts. They're loud, they cuss, and they're dangerous.'

'That's what you see,' Reggie shouts back, 'because you're a racist bigot.'

'I don't give a fuck what you say. All I know is that my granddaughters now can't even play in the park across their street because of all the black thugs who wanna hurt them.'

'You!' Reggie threatens, pushing back his chair. 'You!'

Quickly, I reach for Reggie, afraid that he'll do something rash, but instead he jabs his finger back in the direction of the other man's jabbing finger.

'Reggie,' I call as he storms out. 'What about Pearl?'

'She'll be fine,' he shouts. 'Plenty of white folks here to make sure she's okay.'

'Reggie,' I call again, getting up to follow.

'What,' he snaps, shaking my hand off his shoulder. 'Look, I'm sorry. I'm sorry,' he says, turning reluctantly to face me.

'No,' I tell him. 'You're not the one who should be apologizing.'

18

Normally I would've ignored the old man with his racist vitriol. I know there's no point in trying to talk sense to men like that and yet something about that morning made me lose my cool. Maybe it was because Pearl kept singing her silly songs, maybe because Morayo had joined our table and I was finding it impossible to have a proper conversation with her above the singing and Donna's interruptions. Maybe just because I was hungry. But probably it was the combination of all of the above and my fondness for the chef that made me snap when the old man announced, loud enough for the whole dining room to hear, that certain people are just born irresponsible and that there was something inherently wrong with 'their culture'. This was how the old man explained the chef's absence: categorizing not just the chef but also all black people as irresponsible and uncivilized. I was so angry that I might have struck the man had Morayo not intervened.

I left early that day and then skipped meals for the rest of the week so as not to see him again. And because of this, because I'd missed last night's birthday dinner, I'd missed Morayo's birthday.

Days earlier, when I'd first noticed that it was Morayo's birthday, I had decided to find her a book. I'd gone to the library, thinking that if I saw something good then I'd simply take it and give it to her as my gift. Nobody much used the library, so I reasoned it wouldn't hurt for a book or two to be put to good use in this way, put in the hands of someone who really appreciated them. I even remembered some of the African writers that Morayo had mentioned and looked first for these, but finding none I looked for something different. There were plenty of Agatha Christies in the library, which brought back fond childhood memories. But these, I knew, wouldn't be good enough for a woman of Morayo's sophistication. Not for an English professor. There was a biography of Mother Teresa, which Pearl would've liked, but I wasn't sure how Morayo felt about biographies. Besides, such a book might be depressing and I'd decided that whatever I chose needed to be uplifting and preferably literary, like a Nobel Prize winner. That was why when I spotted *Dear Life,* I knew I'd found the right one. It was a new book, so I figured that Morayo probably wouldn't own it yet. Even if she did, she would surely approve of my choice. So I'd taken the book and put it away in Pearl's bedside drawer. And now, I retrieve it.

Nobody answers when I knock, so I try again.

'Hello,' I call, but still no answer, so I contemplate leaving the book by her door. I don't have a card to go with it, so how will she know it's from me? It's still early, only 8 p.m., so I quietly nudge the door open, just to make sure. The room is silent and the door to the right, leading to her bathroom, is open. The lights are off and I'm about to leave when I peer around the door. We're both surprised but she obviously more than me because she starts to scream and soon others come running and the room fills quickly with people.

'What happened?' the staff ask, accusingly.

'I don't know, I really don't know,' I insist.

Later, she comes looking for me and knocks gently on Pearl's door.

'I'm sorry,' she says.

Her arms, I notice, are clutching a book, but it's not the one that I got for her. 'It's okay,' I tell her, for what else am I supposed to say. It's awkward enough with Pearl trying to sleep and the two of us having this whispered conversation in the hallway.

'I know you're upset,' Morayo says, holding my gaze, 'and I'm sorry. I'm very sorry. I didn't mean to cause a scene. It wasn't logical, I know, but I'd like to try to explain.'

'You don't have to,' I say, but Morayo persists.

'Do you remember, the other day, when I read from the notes that I'd made in this book?'

I shake my head.

'You know, when I brought it to dinner. Do you remember? And I read a little bit to Pearl.'

Now I remember.

'Well I skipped a few bits – so here, please,' she offers me the book. 'I'd like to give this to you because it's easier for me to share it this way.'

I hesitate.

'No,' she says, taking the book back and looking down at where she lets it dangle by her side. 'I should just tell you.' She brings the book back up clutching it closely against her chest. 'Years ago,' she says, looking at me, 'someone, a neighbour, came to my front door.' She pauses, but doesn't look away this time. 'I didn't suspect anything. I trusted him and let him in. But I shouldn't have. And that's why.'

'I'm very sorry to hear that,' I say. 'I'm sorry.'

'No, it's fine,' she shakes her head and turns to leave.

'Morayo!'

She stops and looks back.

'If I may, if you don't mind, can I still read what you wrote?'

I read it while waiting for the bus. 'Your body,' it began, 'seated at your desk with head resting as it thinks between the palms of your hands. Books on your desk, pencils wedged into the thick afro of your hair. Fingers tap softly at the keyboard. Remembering. Your body, shaking in uncontrollable spasms, wracked with memories of your mother who once floated in a bath of blood.' *God*, I gasp, stopping to reread before I continue. 'Your body on the toilet, arms wrapped tightly around knees remembering the menstrual flow and the drips that made red rings in the toilet bowl beneath. Your body constipated. Your mother telling you, 'this is the way childbirth will feel.' Your body unsuspecting when opening the door to welcome the neighbour. Your body fighting. Flailing. Being flailed. Your body in hospital, exposed, and shamed. Your body shaking in uncontrollable spasms, wracked with memories.'

'I'm sorry,' I mutter, 'I'm so sorry.'

'Your body,' I whisper later that night as I lie in bed, returning to thoughts of my childhood. To my body as a thirteen-year-old in Georgetown, British Guiana, discovering girls. To my body learning the hard way that one must never fall in love with a governor's daughter, no matter how close one might feel to the family. My body was told by the governor that I was a coolie; that I must never, ever, set eyes on his daughter, Rose, for she was white and I, my body, was not white. But because I was proud and because I needed to save face, my body, in protest, had gone to that part of town known as the 'nigger yard' to prove to my friends that I was over the governor's daughter; that I really couldn't care less. But above all, my body went there to make Rose jealous. Years later, my body with muscle memory reminds me not to fall in love with another white woman. But then I meet Pearl, and what do I do? My body should have known better. It should have known that Pearl's children would be suspicious of a black man with little money wanting to marry their mother. I shouldn't have been surprised when the children disowned their mother on account of me, but I was. And it was this that my body so clearly remembered, the other day, when the old man began to rant. My body knowing that when the man spoke of his fears for his granddaughters, he was speaking of my body in the way that white men have spoken of black men's bodies for millennia. As threats. As rapists. So earlier, when the only black woman in the Home recoiled from my body in a fit of screaming, my body had felt crushed and humiliated all over again. But now my body understood. 'I understand, Morayo, I do.'

19

For several days, Reggie and I kept asking after Toussaint, wondering what had happened to him. In some ways, having someone else to worry about eased the awkwardness that still hovered between us. But nothing more was heard from Toussaint. The regular chef came back and life at Good Life returned to normal, as normal as normal could be in a place like this. And then when I heard that I was finally leaving, I gave Reggie my phone number and he gave me his. We promised to stay in touch.

I felt relieved to be going home even though I was anxious about what I might find upon my return. Sunshine and an occupational therapist would be accompanying me. The occupational therapist was there to assess whether it was safe for me to live on my own. So I steeled myself, knowing that both would be observing me closely when we got home.

The first thing I looked for were my books. I'd been dreading this and sure enough, just glancing around the apartment, my heart sank. The only books I could see were those on the shelves and they were so neatly arranged that it looked like my apartment was being staged, as though someone was getting ready to sell it. Was this something else that Sunshine hadn't told me? My heart started to race. There were gaps in between the books where ornaments had been placed – a vase here, a photograph there. All the books were arranged by size: the fat cookbooks sat next to the dictionaries and the slim poetry books were nestled in between the children's books. Sunshine was watching me and asked me if I was okay. 'I'm okay,' I said, biting my lip. Then Sunshine and the OT left me for a moment to inspect the bathroom for handrails and other safety features. I snatched the car keys from where someone had placed them on the kitchen counter and let myself out. In the lobby I met Li Wei who handed me the latest stack of letters. He didn't know that I'd been away and, as he searched in the crevices of his postman's bag for any additional envelopes addressed to me, he told me that his son was now a doctor.

'Just like you!' he said, finally looking up and then noticing my tears. 'Doctor!' he exclaimed. 'What's wrong?'

But I didn't want him to see me crying so I waved goodbye, apologizing as I hurried off.

I sat for some moments, tears rolling silently down my cheeks. I was happy to be back, of course I was. I was even happy to see how tidy the apartment looked, despite the missing books; but it was the emptiness that frightened me, made worse by all these cards – more personal notes and cards than I'd received in years. From France, from

India, from Nigeria, and from friends I never thought I'd hear from again. I could hear my father's voice saying, 'Look what magic your seventy-fifth birthday has brought! Think of how fortunate you are, Morayo.' And yet all these friends were so far away. They weren't friends with whom I could share my daily life. And as for my shelf friends, as much as I loved them, they weren't real friends either. I put Buttercup into gear and set off, not knowing where, just that I was going away and speeding. I switched on the radio and found the Bee Gees singing 'Stayin' Alive' so I raised the volume and wound down my window. I knew that I wouldn't pass my next driving test. But I was, 'Stayin' alive, stayin' alive. Ah, ha, ha, ha stayin' alive.' I took Oak Street headed for the freeway, towards the airport maybe. I wanted to drive fast. To close my eyes and feel the wind whip against my face and then drive faster and faster. When I was younger, I used to dream of going so fast that I'd lose control. That I'd drive head on into something so hard – a brick wall or an armoured truck – where the force of sudden impact would kill me, instantly. I had dreamt of a swift ending to what was once the pretence of my marriage and later the struggles of living alone while trying to make ends meet on a teacher's salary. And here I was, now back to these old, familiar, destructive thoughts when I spotted the homeless woman. Or perhaps it was her backpack and the dog that I saw first, before I recognized the thin arms with the head slumped forward. I slowed down, drove around the block and got back to where she was sitting by the side of the road. I parked and went over to her.

'You okay?' I asked.

20

It takes me some minutes to reply cos when this woman asks if I'm okay, it makes me wanna cry. That someone would see me, stop, park their car and then come ask me if I was okay, I didn't expect that, you know.

First of all, I'm having my period today. Second of all, my car got towed. And third of all, I'm love sick. But I don't tell this woman any of that shit. I mean she might be a kind Samaritan, but I still don't know her from Adam. And besides, her eyes are red so it looks like she's been crying too. So I just tell her about my dad. That it's been two years since he's been gone and that this is his birthday weekend as well as Jerry Garcia's. And then I say that they're up in heaven together and my father's teaching Jerry how to play golf, and Jerry and my dad are playing music together – cos my father knew what a Deadhead I was, you know. And then I start laughing cos the image of that, my dad and Jerry, well that makes me happy. And it makes her laugh too. I mean everything is relative, you know.

And if there are people that think their stuff is better than mine because they have a musician as a husband or a boyfriend, then so be it, you know. But at the end of the day we all have to ask ourselves, what did I do for myself? Each of us in on a journey, so like, did you take yourself out on a retreat somewhere, alone, and get to soul-search your own sense of self? Or, you know, can you go anywhere by yourself, you know? And I've proven to myself, yogic-ly, that I can do this, you know. So no, I tell her, when she asks. I don't have a home. But I'm doing fine. I have my car (well not exactly cos it's towed right now) but normally I do. And it's kind of her to offer me her own car. I'm not sure she actually *means* it, but her car wouldn't be big enough for me anyway, not for all my stuff.

Do I feel safe? As a woman? Well I don't think about it, I tell her. If you put that vibe out there it's gonna attract that. So I just don't put that unsafe vibe out there. I know I'm surrounded by a lot of love out here. There's a lot of us out here and we take care of each other. I can hear, 'Don't worry' and stuff like that. I can hear it through the trees, we have a good relationship and they move. They have a pulse. Any living thing has a pulse so I don't fear. No. You can feel the vibes. I have other brothers and sisters that are closer to me than blood. You know? Without a struggle there is no progress. It's what my new motto is. I'm only living in the moment. I know I want to start doing yoga again but I don't wanna go to these classes where everybody's dressed to the nines. It's not the same anymore. I belong to the Y but don't take those classes.

I just stretch on my own and stuff like that. I'm learning to let go of things.

And I guess that the woman likes what I'm saying because she tells me that I'm an inspiration and that she's trying to let go of things too. Then she asks me what I'm reading and she smiles when she sees my book on Africa. She says she knows the owner really well, like maybe they were friends or something, so I have to explain how I found the damn thing in case she thinks that maybe I took it without asking permission or something. Then she tells me that she used to be an English professor and maybe she wants me to go back to school. But what I really wanna do is get married, you know. Find a good man. And she listens to me, like really listens to me, and I almost wanna ask if she'd be my grandmother, like my spiritual grandmother cos she has this calm about her and just talking to her makes me feel better. And then she wants to know about my tattoos.

Which one you wanna know about? I ask her. Well, this one is a yoga, I explain. I thought it was beautiful and the letters meant a lot to me. And so when my father died, I'm like, Dad, where should I put it? And all of a sudden my hand went down to the ankle, so how appropriate that was, you know. You have to pay attention to signs because they're there, you know. It's an easy thing. This one is because I love the Zen, cos I want to practice more. This one is in Chinese and it says, 'The best is yet to come.' That's a song my father loved. This one is my middle name, Rachel, which means 'little lamb' in Hebrew, and I put it with a lion because I see myself as a lion too. This one is stolen from Angelina Jolie, tribal. Yeah, I copied. This is a clothing line, Free People. This one's a necklace, and the one on my wrist is a scarf. Clothing. Yeah, I love fashion. I mean not fashion-fashion but just putting good things together. 'Like you,' I tell her, cos I love all her colours and the turban in her hair. She tells me she has lots of fabrics from Africa. Should we have a fashion business together? Sure! I tell her. I'd love that. So I give her my number and she gives me hers and she tucks the paper into her bra, and I like that, so I do the same.

21

'Well Buttercup, you're my lion, aren't you,' I say, thinking of the woman's tattoo while caressing the car's gearstick. 'Maybe I should've named you lion.' I downshift to hear her roar. Buttercup was what my mum used to call me, did I ever tell you that? And now I'm twice as old as mum ever was. But we've aged well together, haven't we, Buttercup? You looked a little extravagant when I first bought you but now we almost blend in, don't we? You're still not old though, compared to me. But sometime soon, once the driverless cars arrive, even you'll be ancient. What do you make of that? Free, free at last?

So where to now, Buttercup? Do we drive off, into the sunset, or do we go back to visit Mr Reggie? Soon I might not be able to drive, you know. At least that's what the DMV's saying. How would you feel about having another owner? Reggie might be a better driver than me. He certainly sees better than I do. Might not scuff your rims when he parks. What do you think? Do you think he's sitting out there on that little bench of his? He might be puzzled if we turned up right now.

'Missing this place, already?' he'll ask.

'No,' I'll have to reply, 'but I've missed you. And Pearl. And Bella. Especially you.' Then maybe I'll tell him that I dreamt about him. I'll tell him that we danced the bossa nova to the Ferry Building where we ambled along, sampling Frog Hollow peaches and Early Girl tomatoes at the Farmers' Market. That he bought each of us an ice-cream cone wrapped in a paper napkin, and that we sat by the bay in the afternoon sun eating our sweet treats. I licked my fingers to catch the melted drops of honey lavender and salted caramel; while Pearl, who'd turned hers upside down to see what would happen, had lost her raspberry swirl and crunched contentedly on what remained of the cone. Then I'll tell him that my dream changed cities and I was back in Lagos with you, Buttercup. We'd taken Toussaint there for his first trip to the motherland. We were driving back from the airport when we got lost en route to cousin Remi's house. I was driving round and around in circles and didn't know where I was going until someone peered through my window and told me I'd gone blind. But I'm not going blind, am I, Buttercup? 'Come on, baby, we can make this light!' I down shift to third and I hear you roar back. 'Well done, my lion,' I smile, glancing in the rear-view mirror to see how many cars we've left behind. 'One, two, three, four!' I laugh. This will be a great drive. I can just feel it in my bones. 'Come on now, Buttercup, let's make this next light! Let's overtake this slowpoke in front of us. Come on baby, gimme what you got.' I rev the engine, sit up tall, and roaring, we go.